WHAT
shines
FROM IT

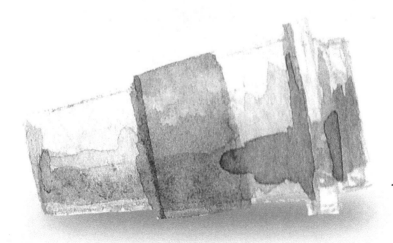

Electric Book
Award Winner

WHAT shines FROM IT

SARA RAUCH
stories

Alternating Current Press
Boulder, Colorado

What Shines from It
Sara Rauch
©2020 Alternating Current Press

Alternating Current
Boulder, Colorado
alternatingcurrentarts.com

ISBN: 978-1-946580-11-5
First Edition: March 2020

"Sara Rauch sneaks up on you with these stories, which seem so perfectly quiet before leveling you with their emotional wallop. These are people we know, or wish we did, people we pull for, hope for, and Rauch's rare mastery of subtlety, and an eye just slightly, but exquisitely, off-kilter, draws us into their lives as if they were our own. Way beyond promising, it's these stories themselves that flat-out shine. Sara Rauch is the real deal."

—Pete Fromm,
author of *A Job You Mostly Won't Know How to Do*

"*What Shines from It* is a classic story collection made contemporary. Familiar plots and settings become refreshed with new angles, and stories that appear placid reveal tremendous depth and nuance. The characters in these stories are complex, tender, and deeply human."

—Eric Shonkwiler,
author of *8th Street Power & Light*

"In Sara Rauch's vivid, tender collection, she dissects the mundane to suss out the figments and phantoms her characters try, mightily, to escape, and doesn't give them an inch. In quiet moments—when they're on the brink, relationships teetering, strangers clutching one another, hungry in all ways—they're held accountable and often left asking where they go from here. And yet, at the center of each of these stories is a bright yearning, a desire to be understood, the question of how to piece ourselves back together after tragedy or heartache or even amid the splendid ordinary. This is a remarkable collection that seeks to catalog the triumphs and agonies of everyday life—an elegantly crafted debut, both empathetic and stirring."

—Robert James Russell,
author of *Mesilla* and *Sea of Trees*

"From the California coast to Midtown Manhattan, Sara Rauch's stories situate us alongside an unforgettable cast of up-and-comers and down-and-outers. These punchy tales amplify quiet moments of grace in between tragedies. *What Shines from It* is a deeply moving and momentous debut."

—Ryan Ridge,
author of *New Bad News*

"The stories in Sara Rauch's *What Shines from It* are lit from within: they glow with intelligence, pathos, and startling insights into the human tragicomedy. This is an extraordinary debut from a writer who has, I daresay, a long and distinguished career ahead of her."

—Christine Sneed,
author of *Little Known Facts* and *The Virginity of Famous Men*

"*What Shines from It* tells stories of couples coming together and falling apart—sometimes at once. You'll find no Hollywood theatrics here, just keenly observed tales of characters and relationships that, like the gold-seamed vase in "Kintsukuroi," show their cracks. With intelligence and grace, Sara Rauch illuminates the beauty in brokenness and the eternal union of love and loss."

—Jennifer Wortman,
author of *This. This. This. Is. Love. Love. Love.*

Table of Contents

for the ghosts

A wound gives off its own light
surgeons say.
If all the lamps in the house were turned out
you could dress this wound
by what shines from it.

—Anne Carson,
The Beauty of the Husband

WHAT shines FROM IT

Secondhand

First morning in our apartment we've got nothing to eat but the egg rolls we nabbed from Dan's freezer before we decamped to pick up the keys. I dig out a plate, but there's no microwave, no dishtowels or potholders, and I burn myself when I try to take them out of the oven. My goddammit brings Jacob from the other room, and he turns on the tap, sticks my hand beneath it.

The water doesn't get cold. White welts streak across all four fingertips. Jacob uses his T-shirt to pull the plate out of the oven.

We need an oven mitt, I say.

Wait for these to cool a little, Jacob says. Don't want to burn your mouth, too. He touches his index finger to my lips.

And Band-Aids, I say.

Jacob pulls a piece of paper out of his back pocket. This list is getting mighty long, he says.

The kitchen's the bigger of the two rooms, and through the doorway is our pile of stuff: three suitcases, a hiking backpack, two boxes of books, two boxes of CDs, sleeping bags, and pillows. Bob Marley's singing, I wanna love ya and treat you right, I wanna love ya, every day and every night. When I told Jacob I wanted to stay in Santa Barbara, he got all serious and asked, Are you sure? Yes, I said. After a summer on the road, I'd made up my mind. It took two months, crashing on a mildewed futon on Jacob's friend Dan's porch, for us to find this place.

If I was dreaming of a life of bikinis and salt-tousled hair and surfboards and endless sun and big windows for all that light to pour into, what I got was a full-time job and old shag carpet, peeling linoleum, front steps covered with the neighbors' junk. We do have two big windows, but they only magnify how dirty everything is.

The shower water proves as lukewarm as the kitchen tap, though I twist the knob all the way and wait before getting in. Which gives me time to stare out the bathroom window, into the courtyard, at the piles of rusty lawn furniture and bicycles.

But it's our own place—I don't have to wear flip-flops in the bathroom or share with four guys. Even if I do have to apply my makeup in the kitchen, compact propped against a mug, because there's no mirror in the bathroom. No sink, either.

I pull the least-wrinkled dress I can find over my head in the back hallway—no one would cover my closing shift— one-handed, the same way I just did my makeup, the same way I'm fumbling with the belt. The blisters are killing me. If I don't hurry, I'll be late.

Does this look okay? I ask Jacob.

He's in the room that isn't the kitchen (the realtor called it the bedroom-slash-living-room) tacking a tapestry to the wall, humming along to the music. I have to ask twice and then poke him in the ribs before he realizes I'm talking.

Smokin', he says.

Not exactly the look I'm going for, I say.

How about a quickie? he says.

We don't even have a bed.

Who needs a bed?

I want a bed, I say. Tomorrow.

Tomorrow you can relax, Jacob says. Because I'm going to unpack everything tonight.

He doesn't have a job yet—the lease is in my name, though he came up with the cash for first, last, and security. I'll probably come home to the bong and the scale and the Ziplocs unpacked, sleeping bags unrolled in a corner, CDs in a perilous stack by the stereo. If I'm lucky, our clothes hanging in the closet.

That's sweet, I say. Are you going to make dinner, too?

Anything for my pretty shop girl, he says.

It's not a bad job, I say.

We hit three mattress places in a row, and in the last Jacob says, I don't want to spend so much on something we can't easily move with.

We signed a six-month lease, I say.

And then what? he says.

How about a futon? We can roll it up.

Eh, he shrugs. If it ain't broke, why fix it?

My back's going to be broke if we don't get a mattress, I say.

He laughs. Let's give it a few weeks. Then we can reevaluate.

You seriously want to sleep on the floor?

He averts his tropical-ocean-blue eyes, and all the air goes out of me. My day off's almost over; my stomach growls —I want a bed, not a debate about a bed.

Fine, I say. Fine. We'll wait.

On the way home, Jacob says, I just need to stop for a pickup.

I opt to stay in the car. Too bad I don't have a magazine—it always takes longer than he says it will.

Later, we'll sit on the kitchen floor and weigh out the half-pound into eighths and quarters. There's a certain rhythm that I like to these known quantities of measurement. How tidy and quiet the process. And how Jacob rubs my neck when we're finished. He'll call for takeout, and I'll pack the baggies into the cigar boxes, stash them in the closet. What happens after this, I steer clear of.

Jacob and I wait on the front steps for Dan.

I'm starving, I say.

Nothing to eat here, Jacob says. He can go entire days without eating, like he's some sort of monk. His focus is elsewhere, his hands in motion, constructing some new world only he can see. He does this when he's anxious, and when he's daydreaming, too. I can't tell which it is right now.

No kidding, I say.

Dan not being where he says he'll be when he says he'll

be there is nothing new. But he's a good guy, one of Jacob's oldest friends, and we need his truck so we don't have to pay for delivery. I saw the place on Milpas last week—used mattresses, cheap—and Jacob agreed to check it out.

I walk down the driveway and circle our car—my car, really. Maybe we can rope it to the top.

We don't have rope, Jacob says.

I'll go to the hardware store, I say.

Why the rush, Jacob says. They're not going to sell out of mattresses.

It's like he enjoys sleeping on the floor, like we're on some unending adventure. Someday, he says, we'll tell our kids about this, and they won't believe it. Our kids? Uh-huh. The ones we're going to have after we travel the world and Jacob gets a respectable job and we buy a fixer-upper somewhere beautiful. The other morning, I complained about my back hurting, and he said sleeping on the floor was good for it. That the heels I wear to work are the culprit.

Another hour goes by. This is ridiculous, I say, and Jacob says, You know how he is, and I do, so I walk to a food cart on Cliff Drive and buy two tacos and sit on the curb and eat. A half-mile down glimmers the long stretch of Pacific. The beaches are officially closed because the water is full of hepatitis. When I asked one of my friends at work, she said, Happens around this time every year. Something about the currents—you can still go to the beach; it just means the city isn't responsible if you get sick. A risk Jacob and I take most nights—getting my feet wet and sandy never fails to thrill me. You can see the offshore platforms dotting the horizon, and our soles are splotched black with tar.

Dan's truck is in the driveway when I get back. He says, Yo, Sam, where've you been?

No one here calls me by my full name—Samantha—and I don't mind, but the shortening is like a dress that doesn't quite fit.

Eating, I say.

You didn't get us anything? Jacob says.

I climb into the truck between Jacob and Dan.

Dan says, Let's grab something now.

Jacob says, Dude, let's get the bed. Then I'll buy you a burrito.

We get to the mattress place, and the first thing out of Dan's mouth is, You're going to buy a used mattress?

Certified, Jacob says, waving both of his hands at the window where the word is stenciled in graffiti script. He squints in that suspicious way of his.

Dan looks at me, and I look at him, and I know what he's thinking. But Dan's got divorced parents constantly trying to one-up each other. He sleeps on a pillowtop, memory foam, plusher-than-plush king-size.

I say, Anything's better than the floor, right?

Dan shrugs. He already thinks I'm a novelty because I once changed a flat tire on his truck—his housemates think the same because I never complained about sleeping on their porch or about the *Playboys* stacked on the back of their toilet.

The store is dark and smells like the underside of a mushroom. The salesman—shorter than me, in polyester pants—tells Jacob that Certified means the mattresses are properly sanitized according to state law. Sanitized with what? Jacob asks. Steri-Fab, the guy says, all confidence and yellow teeth. I'm about to start testing our options when Jacob touches my arm and says, Let's go outside for a sec.

What? I say.

Jacob's hands flail, bleach-white in the bright sun, and I blink hard to get my eyes to adjust.

We can't get the mattress here, he says.

Why not?

Jacob looks at Dan and back at me and says, Sammy, they're poisoned. We can't sleep on a poisoned mattress.

Dan says, He's got a point.

But— A knot forms in my throat, and I swallow it back.

Jacob's fists clench midair. Steri-Fab? Who the hell even knows what that is.

It's state-approved, I say.

Jacob grabs both my hands. Exactly, it's like smallpox blankets.

Are you kidding? I yank free from his grip.

Dude's watching from the window, Dan says, pointing, and sure enough, there's the sales guy, though he ducks back when we all look.

Let's get lunch, Jacob says.

I already ate, I say.

Jacob and Dan get into the truck. I stand there, arms crossed. Except for the gulls strutting, the parking lot is empty. The guy comes back to the window, sees me, scoots away. I'm about to walk back inside when Dan leans across Jacob and says, Sam, we'll go to my place right now and get the futon. You can have it.

I don't need a consolation prize, I say.

Dan shrugs, shifts the truck into gear. I'm so hungry, he says. We can come back.

I get in and climb over Jacob to the middle seat.

This isn't worth arguing about, Jacob says, putting his arm around me.

Looks like I'll be locking my chastity belt till further notice then.

Hoo boy. Dan whistles. Sometimes I'm really glad I'm single.

Liars, Jacob says, and Dan laughs.

We sit at the kitchen table, music loud, and I'm drinking coffee and shivering, looking through the doorway at the sleeping bags lying there like abandoned snakeskin. Beneath them I've built a nest of quilts from the thrift store.

We've acquired a reclining chair—Jacob rolled it home on his skateboard—and a coffee table. Dishtowels, a frying pan, a hook to hold our keys, a spatula and cheese grater, one of those ugly metal hanging baskets for garlic and onions. Everything second- or third- or fourth-hand. Jacob even brought home an aloe and a jade plant from one of his regulars. They droop on the kitchen windowsill. Every day I cross my fingers I'll come home to a mattress, and every day I don't.

Do you think it's true what the realtor said about none of the apartments here having heat? I ask Jacob. Do Dan and them have heat?

Dunno, Jacob says. On his plate is a half-eaten piece of toast and a half-smoked joint. His typical breakfast.

Because I'm freezing, I say. Feel the tip of my nose.

I can think of a few ways to warm up, Jacob says. He slips his hands beneath my sweatshirt and I shriek, laughing, wiggling away, spilling coffee all over the floor. See, Jacob says, warmer already.

His hands linger over the goosebumps rising on my back, and it calms me, a little. My mind's all jumbled lately—*you're not from here, are you?* and *don't make all the same mistakes I did* and *be home soon* and *this is some killer shit* and *jewelry numbers are down* and *next week, next week, next week*—but it goes quiet when I match my mouth to Jacob's. Afterward I wonder if this is the only common language we share.

We drive north to spend the holidays with Jacob's mom, who stuffs us full of lentil loaf and vegetarian gravy and root vegetables and kale and takes us to a Yule ceremony.

She asks what my favorite part of living in Santa Barbara is, and I tell her about feeding the seagulls—how they circle around me, cawing, swooping to snatch the bread I buy for them, that moment right before their feet touch the sand.

The art of landing, she says.

She's a midwife, and she spends Christmas Eve out catching a baby. Her word: catching. Like the baby is rocketing in from some other world, and there'll be Jane's hands, ready to soften the impact. I wish I had a pair of hands like that.

The whole visit Jane's eyes are on me, like I'm hurtling through the air myself, like she's readying her position. I try to pretend I don't notice, and when she asks if I'm taking care of myself, I tell her I'm just tired. She says, Maybe your iron is low. She prescribes more leafy greens, but still she watches.

I sleep till eleven every morning we're there, except the last day. Lying in Jacob's old twin bed, I hear Jacob say, We're fine, and then Jane: Just take it. Buy Samantha a bed. It's not like she's asking for a diamond.

But we get home and still no bed. I wait. What's another week? Two. Three—

Until the night we're cooking dinner, and I'm watching the water boil, and I can't stand it anymore: We need a bed. I don't know why this is such a thing with you.

And Jacob, knife poised over a tomato, says, It's not a thing.

Don't play dumb—I'm tired of this.

And you think a mattress will help? he says.

I pick up the nearest bowl and fling it at the floor.

Jacob jumps a little and says, What the—

It's a bed, Jacob. Why is that so fucking hard for you to understand? I start to cry—I don't want to—I can't help it.

He puts the knife down and stoops to pick up the pieces of the bowl. We're both barefoot. He gets the trash, throws the bigger pieces in, gets the broom. I stand there, sniffling. Like a girl.

He puts his arms around me, strokes my hair.

I should've kept my word, I say.

He steps back, takes my chin in his hand. About what?

Not letting you touch me till we got a mattress.

He sighs, and my whole body stiffens at that sigh, and then he says, I'll get you a mattress. I'll get it tomorrow.

I'm pregnant, I say, and he steps back like it's contagious.

We stare at each other, in this awful way, all my tears gone, and what I've suspected for over a month, and known for sure since yesterday, settles around us.

What about—? he says.

What about it? It's not foolproof, I say. But who's the fool here, him or me?

What are we gonna do, he says, and he sits down.

What I am going to do, I say, is go to the clinic, and—

We should talk about it, Jacob says. He takes my hand, tries to pull me closer.

I already made the appointment. There's nothing to talk about.

Jacob knows this, I know he knows this, but his head sags. He flexes and unflexes his hands—they're so elegant, like bird wings—and says, Just tell me what you need.

I need a bed, I say, and he nods, like maybe he finally

gets it. Not that it matters right now. All the padding in the world won't make this landing any softer.

⏝

Jacob holds the front door, so I go in first. There, in place of our sleeping bags, is a bed. A mattress and frame and quilt and matching pillowcases.

Big, I say.

He goes over and pulls back the covers. He says, Get in.

And even though my whole body aches, even though I'm crampy and bleeding and more exhausted than I've ever been in my entire life, I don't move.

Jacob's face betrays nothing like sadness or shame. Do you like it? he says.

Where'd it come from?

He walked through the protesters with me, sat in the waiting room, still clutches the sheet of care instructions. *If you develop a fever. If you bleed through more than three thick pads in three hours. If you pass gray, green, or white tissue.*

Dan brought it, Jacob says.

He bought us a bed?

I bought it, Jacob says. He delivered it.

Take the antibiotics you were sent home with. Take over-the-counter painkillers as needed.

I know I should say thank you. But my mind's stuck on the story Jane told me over the holidays, about a mother of hers whose baby stopped moving inside at seven months. How the woman carried it to term, how the labor dragged on, how the baby arrived blue-lipped, with ten delicate fingers and ten delicate toes. And I think of how long the woman waited, just to have that still form placed in her arms.

Jacob says, You need rest.

He unlaces my shoes and pulls my feet out of them. I get in between the sheets. Blue. They smell brand-new, creased in perfect rectangles.

He says, Do you need anything? and when I shake my head, he lies down behind me.

Resume your normal activities the following day.

You made the right choice, he says.

Avoid anything that causes pain.

You'll be a good mother someday, he says.

You're not helping, I say.

He loops his arm around me, rests his hand on my belly.
But it causes pain, and I move away.

Answer

A t the far end of the bar, the blonde sat with a book splayed open, sipping a clear fizzy drink through a cocktail straw, tucking a bright yellow curl behind her ear. She reminded Seth of the goldfinch he often saw perched in the crabapple tree near his kitchen window. Besides the bartender, a silent man with smooth cheeks in a black gabardine vest and newsie cap, and the finch girl, the bar was empty. But it was one in the afternoon, and Seth didn't have anywhere else to be. He'd been wandering the East Village for almost an hour after his brunch meeting when the carved wooden sign caught his eye.

The girl did not acknowledge Seth's presence when he sat down three stools over from her. He ordered a scotch neat and a Brooklyn Amber. In the age-speckled mirror that hung over the bottles, Seth watched the girl turn a page and reach up to tuck her hair behind her ear again. The bartender brought Seth's beer and scotch. It was a generous pour in a cloudy lowball glass. The bartender didn't make eye contact and retreated to the other end of the bar.

Seth gulped the scotch and slid over two stools, leaving one empty between the girl and himself. Hi, he said.

I'm not interested, she said, glancing up from her book. Her eyes were the color of blue sea glass.

But I haven't asked a question, he said.

I'm going to save you the bother.

Are you sure? he asked.

The girl sighed and rested a forefinger on the page. I'm pretty sure, she said.

What are you reading? he asked.

She flipped the book shut. *Light Years* by James Salter.

Never heard of it, Seth said. He read the newspaper spottily, and *National Geographic* regularly, and little else.

She reopened the book, pressing down hard along the center so the pages lay flat, and began to read again.

Seth said, Can I buy you a drink?

You're not from the city, are you? she said. Along her jaw ran a serrated scar that disappeared up behind her ear and into her hair.

Different city—Boston, he said, sipping his beer. Well, outside of Boston.

Do the women in Boston respond well to your ineptitude? She looked at him, more with curiosity than annoyance.

Dunno. I've been married for almost a decade. I don't spend much time in bars.

So, what are you doing here? she tilted her face, concealing the scar in shadow.

Business trip, he said.

For? she said.

What's your name?

She regarded him for a second before turning the book over on the bar. The cover was worn, and its edges curled when she moved her hand, which she extended across the empty stool. Liz.

Short for? he said, taking her hand. It was dry and small, its slight heft like the body of a sparrow.

Just Liz.

Liz Short-for-Nothing.

At your service.

Seth Brown. So. Drink?

She raised her eyebrows—very pale, almost invisible—and said, I'll have a vodka tonic. She pronounced *vodka* with a short chirping of the vowels.

The bartender brought her drink. Liz moved onto the empty bar stool, closing the gap. She wore a simple black sweater with a wide boat-neck, and Seth saw a tattoo edging across her shoulders. He couldn't tell what it was, a tree branch maybe, or a vine.

What brings you here on this beautiful Sunday? More

often than not, now, he hated the words that came from his mouth.

My roommate's parents are in town, and I didn't want to have lunch with them. What kind of work do you do? she asked, letting her eyes dart to his wedding band.

The soul-gobbling kind.

That bad, huh? She smiled, revealing very white, very straight teeth.

Insurance. He nodded in the bartender's direction for another beer. Liability and data breach.

Sounds boring.

It is ungodly dull. What do you do?

I work for a nonprofit. Literacy in inner-city schools.

That's noble, he said.

Yeah, but I can barely afford to share a tiny apartment, and I only eat rice and beans.

Money isn't everything, Seth said.

People with money say that a lot, Liz said, bobbing her head and sipping her vodka. What's your wife's name?

Abigail.

Is she in insurance, too?

She takes care of our son.

That's sweet.

It's fine. She seems happy with it.

The door of the bar opened, and two women came in. One had a shaved head, the other wore her hair cropped, but styled like Mia Farrow in *Rosemary's Baby*. The shaved-headed one caught Liz's eye and nodded. Seth thought he saw Liz flinch. She focused on her vodka, stabbing the cocktail straw into the ice.

He said, How long have you lived in the city?

Instead of answering, she lifted her tumbler and drank the vodka down in a smooth gulp. Want to go somewhere else? Liz asked.

Where?

Wherever, she said.

She snapped the book shut, tucked it into her canvas bag, and pulled on her coat. Seth settled the tab. He paid for Liz's first drink, too, the one she'd been almost finished with when he arrived. The bartender brought Seth's change, slid it across the bar—he had tapered fingers, and his nails were short and very clean. Seth left too big a tip, filed the other bills into his wallet.

On their way out, the shaved-headed woman held up her hand in a gesture that looked like both peace offering and wave, and said, Hey, Liz.

Liz did not break her stride. She lifted her hand and said, Hey, before pulling the door open and stepping out onto the sidewalk. Behind her, Seth smiled toward the woman and nodded, but the woman frowned and turned away.

Out on Fifth Street, they stood in awkward pause. Liz was fine-boned but tall, almost as tall as Seth. The upper bricks of the buildings across the street caught the sun. Two doors down, a fire escape decorated with pinwheels and streamers refracted metallic light into the afternoon air. Liz's gaze followed Seth's to the offering of radiance.

She said, Ever been on the Staten Island Ferry?

He shook his head. The sky beyond the bricks was sharp blue, scalloped with cirrus clouds.

How long do you have?

I'm free the rest of the day.

All right, Seth Brown. Let's walk. This is our first real spring day.

He hadn't paid much attention to the weather since his arrival the day before. Sometimes Manhattan felt like an airless dome—not a real ecosystem at all. Early April was the same as December or August, a blurry presence obscured by concrete. But he saw now the purple-headed crocuses budding up from hard-packed dirt, the tiny green shoots emerging from slender branch tips. Liz was beside him ruffling her curls with her hands, waiting for him. Pigeons preened and strutted along the curb, their heads nodding. He said yes.

Liz weaved their way downtown; as they went, the streets and sidewalks narrowed. Seth had no idea where they were until he saw Chinese characters printed across red awnings. They skirted the Canal Street artery—he'd taken Abigail here once, after college, in search of a knockoff Coach bag—until the overcrowded bustle and teetering vegetable carts gave way to stately buildings. The Brooklyn Bridge loomed to their left before Liz cut across a sliver of park and led them into the close alleyways of the financial district.

metal rail as she moved back toward him. When their trajectories reconnected, he saw that her fingernails were chewed to the quick, distinguishable from his own only by their smallness. Liz settled close to him, resting her arm and thigh against his.

I always think about the *Titanic* when I ride the ferry, she said. Like we could go down here. It's grandiose, really—silly to imagine any loss of life in this banal bay.

Grandiose, and entirely possible, Seth said.

Liz laughed and rolled her eyes.

Seth looked up at the clouds now streaking across the sky, dulling its blue to the pale color of a robin's egg. In college, Seth had been a painter, obsessed with mixing colors to match the sky—a seemingly endless task—the sky was a new shade every day, every hour. He rarely studied the sky anymore; there was no time for something so capricious.

Despite the chill blowing off the water, he felt Liz's warmth pressing into his body, felt it seep under his skin and ascend his spine. He wanted to touch her hair, the sunniness of it. Gulls swooped and shrieked, caws carrying through the crystalline air. Seth and Liz stood there, arms and thighs alive against one another, until the boat docked on Staten Island. They disembarked in the tide of passengers, circled around, waited to board again.

They returned to their place on the prow. Across the water, the tip of Manhattan shimmered, tiny and jagged. Missing an essential piece, Seth thought. There would be a new tower—they'd already begun constructing it—a replacement. But there were no new lives for the ones lost, nothing rising in their place.

He worried about his mortgage and marriage and money—these were the necessities of his life, the things that would remain if he were gone—and this bothered him. It bothered him that he'd gone looking for his *Encyclopedia of Birds* one recent afternoon, and unable to find it, had asked Abigail where it was. She said, That old thing? I let Andy bring it to school for a project. Andy, upon questioning, could not recall the book. Seth had said, It's a big book, with a hawk on the cover? Andy had shaken his head, his serious eyes darkening with confusion, and said, I don't remember, Daddy. I'm sorry. Seth had said, It's okay, buddy. It's just a book. It was not essential; the book was easily replaced. But Seth had not yet bought another copy.

He said, I've always wanted to live in Manhattan.

Why?

He thought it odd—he thought *Why not?* He said, It's alive here. There are answers here to questions no one has ever asked.

That's deep, she said.

Don't patronize me.

I'm not.

Their bodies were no longer touching, but she watched him—he felt her eyes as tangibly as he had her upper arm and hip.

She said, Where do you think those answers are?

All around us. Circling the way birds do buildings.

Occasionally crashing into us and bleeding to death on the sidewalk?

He laughed. Maybe these birds don't die against the glass. Maybe they survive the impact. The wind and sun and glare of the water pushed at their faces, made them squint. He liked it. He liked standing next to this woman, the smell of diesel and dirty water mixing with the woodsy aroma of her.

That's romanticizing this place. People who don't live here do it all the time. If you lived here, you would know about homeless men asleep on broiling sidewalks with flies swarming their shit-stained pants. About roaches the size of mice, the creepy sound of their antennae tapping the walls. What it was like to live through the aftermath of the towers —to live with that dust inside you. Buildings are solid, Seth Brown, but even they fall down.

You were here?

I was.

Did you—?

Liz closed her eyes and jerked her head from right to left, just once. Her scar glowed in the fading light. Sharp. Definitive. But yes or no he could not tell. He had not even finished his question.

Have dinner with me? he asked.

What about your wife?

My wife. He thought of Abigail's shiny brown hair in a

ponytail, how rarely she kissed him goodnight. He thought of the pair of boxer briefs he had found stuffed into her nightstand drawer. She must think him so daft.

I don't think your wife would appreciate your taking me to dinner, Liz said.

I'm not going to tell her, Seth said.

Where's your hotel? Liz asked.

Tribeca.

I'm gay, you know.

You could just decline my offer.

I'll think about it.

W hen they were back on Water Street, Liz said, I'll walk with you.

By now, dusk settled between the buildings, the last rays of daylight illuminating windows and softening shadows into inky smudges. He wanted to ask again about dinner, did not want to leave her scent—it was pine, he had figured out, now that they were off the water, pine and something grittier: moss, tree-bark, humus—or the buzzing her proximity created in his body. She was gay. And he was not the sort of man who cheated on his wife. None of it made any sense.

They walked with an inch of space between them, Liz humming. What street is your hotel on? she asked.

Hudson, he said.

And the cross street?

I don't know. I'll recognize it when we get there.

Liz smiled, and he saw then that her first smile, the one over drinks, had been a fake.

Who was that woman? he asked.

Which one? she said.

The one in the bar.

No one, Liz said, and the smile faded. Someone I used to know.

An ex?

An ex of an ex, she said.

Something happened between you?

Something always happens. Her voice went cold, far away.

I suppose it does.

It's different from the straight world.

I don't think it is, he said. His wife, when he came home from work, smelled like the sweat of another man.

And you're some sort of authority on the matter?

No. I just think all relationships are complicated. There was his wife's false cheeriness as she prepared dinner, the way she talked only to Andy at the dinner table.

You know you came into a gay bar?

What about the bartender? he asked.

What about her?

That was a woman? he said and felt suddenly stupid. Of course. The smooth chin, the narrow shoulders and fine hands.

Kylie. Yup.

Seth let out a low whistle. I just thought the sign was clever. He remembered its carved image of a sawed-off tree trunk from which overflowed dozens of little birds, some with bows atop their heads, others adorned with bowties. And I wanted a beer.

Aleta's is a lesbian institution—

How would I know that? he said.

You're a strange duck, Seth Brown.

How was I supposed to know Aleta Alehouse is a gay bar? It's not like there was some rainbow over the door.

Liz glanced at him and raised an eyebrow. You're right. You couldn't have known.

They lapsed into silence—but it was an easy silence, nothing like the one Abigail and he had struck—until he saw the hotel sign appear. It's this one, he said, pointing.

They were in front of a deli, buckets of flowers on display under fluorescent lights. Liz's hair matched the sunflowers. She angled toward him and studied his face before she extended her hand and said, Nice to meet you, Seth Brown.

With her gloves on, her hand no longer had the weightlessness of a sparrow. She felt sturdier, wrapped in protective raiments. Come up for a drink? Seth asked, still holding her hand.

She dropped her eyes and studied her feet. Then she drew a line in front of her with her toe. I won't cross that line, she said, looking up at him.

What line?

You're married.

He nodded, held her stare.

One drink. Then I have to go.

n the hotel room, Liz removed her gloves and jacket and shoes. She was not wearing socks, and had a purple morning glory tattooed over the top of her right foot.

Vodka tonic? Seth offered.

She nodded, sitting on the bed. She used the remote to turn on the TV, flipping to CNN before hitting the mute button. Then she leaned back against the pillows—huge and fluffy, repositioned by housekeeping after Seth had tossed them on the floor—and closed her eyes. Her sharp collarbones jutted upward, visible beneath the drape of her sweater. Seth removed his tie and his work shirt. In his T-shirt, without the required buttons and knots, he fixed the drinks, more vodka than tonic, before sitting on the bed next to Liz.

She opened her eyes, but instead of taking the drink from his hand, she said, I wouldn't have guessed, touching his left forearm, which was covered in tattoos. The Little Owl, she said, tracing the outline of the bird on his inner wrist.

Aleta means *winged one* in Greek, he said.

It's the owner's name, she said, taking her drink from his hand.

They sipped and stared at the TV screen, where the image of a woman kneeling and wailing in a shattered street flashed and disappeared.

There was nothing, Seth knew, watching the etched lines of the woman's contorted face, nothing even remotely interesting about his own suffering, about the question he asked himself as he let his foot relax and rest on Liz's ankle. She did not flinch or move away, kept her eyes on the images on the screen.

Abigail had been sleeping with their neighbor, and Seth had let it go on for over a year. Let it go on while he paid the bills and loved his son and mowed the lawn on Saturdays. Let it go on because there was always food in the refrigerator, and a warm body beside him when he fell asleep at night. What was infidelity in the face of death, of loss? Nothing. A drop in the bucket. Not even large enough to ripple. He knew what he had done wrong: accept as true the respectable adult life that was his McMansion on a cul-de-sac in the suburbs with a woman who wanted nothing more than facials and lawn parties and her child in private school. What he had done wrong was accept the job that paid for it all and let Abigail buy him ties, hundreds of them, every time she needed to give him a gift. The image on the screen flashed to footage of men running, their narrow backs pursued by clouds of smoke and plaster. The banner below read *Air Strikes in Gaza.*

Liz rolled onto her side, balancing her drink on the mattress. Seth shifted toward her and put his hand on her hip.

I've been thinking about leaving New York, she said. Her mouth tipped down.

Why?

Why not? I don't love it here. I'm tired.

Where will you go? Back to Connecticut?

I'll never go back there.

Seth took the vodka from her hand and leaned over her, setting it on the nightstand. His heart thumped against her shoulder; he felt the flutter of her breathing. When he moved back to his spot, her body followed him. He kissed her. She kissed him. She leaned into his chest, wound her arm through his, gripped his hand. Then she ducked her head, so his mouth was on her hairline.

It's been a long time since I kissed a man, she said.

She let her face fall back, and they stared at each other. She kissed him again, leaning in with something akin to hunger. He had not felt it in her before, but now he understood—she was starved. They both were.

How long they kissed, he lost track—his hands in her hair, on her neck, down her back until he was pulling her hips into his, feeling their fragile boniness. She kissed slowly, carefully, against his fervent motions, and said, once, *Gentle*, before closing her eyes to him, before tracing her tongue in a circle around his lips. But when he went to unbutton her jeans, to slip his hand down—she was not wearing underwear, his fingertips met only skin and a wiry brush of hair—she intercepted his hand and said, without hesitation, *No.*

He blinked, and she came into focus, her eyes clouded, her body still in full contact with his but the refusal plain on her face.

I can't, she said. I won't.

But haven't we already—?

Crossed the line, Liz said.

Seth nodded, did not release her from his arms.

One line. But there are others. You must know that.

I don't know. I've never done this before.

I don't believe you, she said.

You should, he said.

My parents disowned me. I told them I like women. I'm not straight. I made that decision a long time ago. This would not be fair. To either of us.

It hurt, to hear the words. He liked kissing her, liked the surrender of her body in his arms, liked her scent and her bravery. Liked, above all else, the possibility of her.

What's it like, he said, to believe in something so fiercely?

It's not belief. It's my identity. But it's like anything else, I guess. You launch yourself into the air and hope you figure it out before gravity gets wind of you. You get up every morning and pretend you know how to keep aloft.

Do you think we're all pretending? Seth thought of the dead chickadee his son had found in the yard last week—black feathers worn away from its cap, the dull, sandy body in Andy's cupped palm. Andy cried while Seth dug a hole in the sodden ground to bury it, and when Seth told Abigail this later, she rolled her eyes and said, *He's so sensitive. It's just a bird.*

To some extent, I do.

And right now?

She rested her forehead on his shoulder and let out a long sigh. Not now. But this isn't real life.

What is it?

It's a moment. It will pass.

Have you tried to talk to your parents—about being gay,

about being happy?

They're spineless bigots.

That's harsh.

They deserve it, Liz said.

My wife doesn't love me anymore, Seth said.

How do you know?

She never looks at me. She's fucking someone else and barely hides it.

So this is revenge? Liz's body shifted almost imperceptibly away from his.

No, not really. I like you, felt pulled toward you in some way.

Why should I believe that? she asked.

You don't have to believe anything. But I'm telling you.

Liz was quiet.

Where will you go? he asked again.

California, maybe. Or the Cape, near the ocean. But maybe I won't leave. Maybe I like the fantasy of someplace else.

I think we all do, Seth said.

There aren't any answers here, Liz said. Any more than there are anywhere. We all live under the same sky.

If that's not romanticizing things, I don't know what is, he said.

Liz stifled a laugh. She said, Now you sound like a New Yorker. There's hope for you yet.

He let his mind trace back across the years to all the shades of color he'd mixed: purple and magenta and orange and every variation of blue and gray. How his neck ached from constantly craning his head, studying up. He wanted to tell her how much he missed it.

Liz's body relaxed into his and after a few minutes, he felt the evenness of her exhales, how her body nestled into itself as she dropped into sleep. He stayed still as her body softened further, as if relieved of some great burden. He bent his neck and rested his face on her hair, inhaling the earthen dustiness of her. The neckline of her shirt gapped, and he saw then the tattoo inked on her shoulders: Wings. Delicate feathers, spread to fly.

Why the sky? everyone had asked him, Abigail included, and he never had an answer.

Addition

Alex kicks shut the cabin's back door, and before she can unzip her coat, her son flies into the room and flings himself into her arms, shouting, We're having popovers for diiiiiiinner!

Rain, I'm right here, Alex says.

We were just wondering where you were, Rose says, gracing the kitchen doorway, flour streaked in her rust-red hair.

Popovers! Rain wiggles away from Alex and races around the family room.

Stopped off at McCusker's. Alex holds up a bottle of wine.

Rough day?

I mashed my thumb. Alex removes her glove, revealing a bloodied and blackening nail.

Rose examines it. Not too bad, she says. But you better soak it. And put some antibacterial on. The oven timer sounds, and Rose turns back to the kitchen.

Alex unzips her jacket. What'd you do today, Rain?

Made a volcano, and a tornado. Rain keeps running around the room.

Are you the tornado? Alex asks.

Rain circles again, his breath coming in puffs.

Rose returns and intercepts him. Calm down. Time to go pick which toys you want for your bath. As soon as Rain is out of earshot, Rose says, We've got trouble.

Oh? Alex pulls off her sweatshirt.

Of the mouse variety, Rose says.

Ah, finally tired of the snow. Should I get traps?

It can wait till tomorrow. Rose gestures toward Rain's bedroom, where he sings a nonsense version of "Baa, Baa, Black Sheep." As long as he doesn't find out.

Secret Mission: Mouse.

Will you give him his bath? I have to finish dinner.

I'll soak my thumb while I'm at it.

If it gets infected, and I have to lance it, you'll be sorry, Rose says. She puts a finger to her lips, goes back into the kitchen. Alex runs the water and has to call Rain three times before he comes into the bathroom.

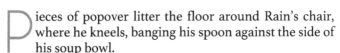

Pieces of popover litter the floor around Rain's chair, where he kneels, banging his spoon against the side of his soup bowl.

Rose grips the stem of her wine glass. Please eat. It's almost bedtime.

No, Rain says.

Rose widens her eyes.

Alex takes the spoon from Rain, says, If you don't finish your dinner, there'll be no story.

Rain pouts, but holds out his hand.

As Alex gives Rain back the spoon, Neuf saunters in, a mouse dangling from his jaws. He drops it onto the linoleum. Rain jumps out of his chair and snatches the body. Mousie!

No, Alex and Rose say in unison.

Rose leaps up and pries the mouse from his hand. You cannot touch that, she says.

You're touching it, Rain says, grabbing for it.

Rose holds it high. It could have a disease. You could get sick.

Rain glares, and jams his thumb into his mouth.

Rose yanks his arm, dislodging the thumb. Clean him, please, she says, pushing Rain toward Alex and sweeping out of the room with the mouse.

Alex lifts Rain to the sink and scrubs his hands with hot water. She doesn't know what to do about his mouth, so she makes him rinse with white vinegar. He gags, his face red.

Time for bed, Alex says. You're tired.

Am not, Rain says, breaking into full wail.

After she gets Rain tucked in, Alex stretches out on the threadbare couch. Rose pokes around in the woodstove, embers popping. She slides in a log and closes the door halfway.

What'd you do with the mouse? Alex asks.

Flushed it, Rose says. She sits near the stove and pulls a hat from her knitting basket, switches on the lamp.

That can't be good for the septic, Alex says.

Rose pulls at a dropped stitch, begins to unravel backward. In the pool of light, her skin glows and her eyelashes cast spidery shadows over her cheeks. Alex wouldn't have thought it possible, but Rose grows more beautiful as she ages, her features not as sharp as when she was dancing, her eyes clearer. She's putting down roots here: taking nursing classes at the community college, turning the garden every spring, homeschooling Rain.

Rose says, I want to talk about—

Can we just have a nice night? Alex says. Her thumb throbs.

I want Rain to have a sibling, Rose says. I thought you wanted that, too.

It's not safe for you to have another baby, Alex says.

He's going to be five soon—I don't want to wait much longer.

You remember what the midwife said.

Never mind the midwife. That's old news. It's you we're talking about—it's safe for you.

Alex sits and looks into the fire. The flames remind her of Rose—her wild hair, her mesmerizing movements.

Every time I mention it, you clam up, Rose says.

I— Alex starts, but claws scrabbling against linoleum and a high-pitched squeaking interrupt her.

In the kitchen, Neuf crouches with a mouse between his two thumbed paws. He whacks it on the head, and it circles like a wind-up toy.

Let's get it outside, Rose says.

It'll just come back, Alex says.

Do you have a better idea? Rose corners Neuf, who has snapped up the mouse and growls, intent on his prize. She grabs him and carries him, mouse in mouth, out the back door.

Alex opens the junk drawer, starts rummaging.

I know you've never wanted to be pregnant, Rose says, returning with Neuf gripped under her arm. And I'd gladly carry another. But I can't.

There must be some sort of trap in here, Alex says, shuffling through rubber bands and screws and packs of cards, a doll arm, matchbooks from restaurants long closed.

Are you going to ignore me? Rose says.

Alex digs out two rusty traps from the back of the drawer. What if *I* can't?

We won't know unless you try.

You almost died giving birth, Alex says. Which is a risk I'm not sure I'm willing to take.

You know how unlikely it is that you'd have the same complications.

Can we deal with the mice and talk about this later?

At some point, not making a decision is a decision, Rose says.

Alex sets the springs. This will have to do for now.

A lex spends all night listening to mice scrabble in the walls. Around dawn, there are two loud snaps, and Alex groans. She goes to the kitchen and opens the curtains and makes coffee. She drinks a cup. She does not want to deal with the mice. She does not want to deal with any of this.

The two squashed mice are small and thin; it bothers her to plop them unceremoniously into the trash. Weak light fills the kitchen as the sun crests the hill behind the cabin. They're just mice, she tells herself, pouring more coffee. That's when she notices the turds: counter, stove, cutting board, sink. She remembers her dad's cheek swelling with infection after he cleaned out the attic before Rose and she moved in five years ago, and her mother's worry that he'd contracted hantavirus, the doctor's repeated assurance that that wasn't the case. How the medicine knocked her dad for a loop and in the end didn't work, the infection landing him in the hospital, pumped full of some aggressive pain-killer-antibiotic cocktail. Alex gets one of Rose's scarves from near the door and, wrapping it around her face, disinfects the surfaces.

Neuf sits on the table, watching.

You, Mr. Nine Lives, are not doing your job. Alex waves the spray-bottle at him. Plus, you're not allowed on the table, she says, and chases him outside.

By the time Rose and Rain wake up, Alex has cleaned everything twice, dressed for work, and stands by the back door watching a group of crows raise their underworld racket at Neuf's stalking presence.

Where are you today? Rose asks. Rain leans against her, thumb in his mouth.

That place in Beckett, Alex says. I'll be home early-ish.

And you'll get the stuff at the store?

If you're not planning on going out.

I'm not, Rose says.

Maman's teaching me about weather today, Rain says. Storms.

Rose pats Rain's head. Natural disasters, she says.

After work, Alex kicks shut the back door—come warmer weather, she needs to refit it—and discovers the cabin empty. She puts the bag of traps in the pantry and grabs a beer, sits on the couch, props her feet up. She wants to sink into the cushions and not move till Monday. The words she's avoided all day—*Unless you try*—whir to life, a circular saw waiting to cut through her objections. No reason she can come up with, and there are many, will cancel out the possibility lying dormant inside her.

The back door opens, and Rain barrels into the room, Ma— Ma— Snow— and leaps into Alex's lap.

Rose shoves the door shut with her hip, slips off her boots and hat. Her hair teeters in a bun on top of her head. She smiles, and Alex smiles back, glad for a ceasefire, even if temporary; *adagio* was, after all, Rose's specialty on stage.

Did you learn about snow? Alex asks.

Rain runs his hands through Alex's hair. Sawdust flies. A storm coming. A big storm.

Again?

They've predicted two, Rose says. One right on top of the other. A couple feet.

How'd I miss that?

Other things on your mind?

Did you bring in wood?

I haven't had a chance, Rose says.

I'll take care of it then, Alex says, pushing up from the couch.

And I'll start dinner. Rose picks up Alex's empty beer bottle.

Rain casts his eyes between them. Can I go with you, Ma? he asks.

Of course. I need your big muscles, Alex says.

Their boots crunch over the rimy, old snow. Dusk edges through the bare trees. Alex carries a flashlight, beaming it onto the padlocked shed door.

Behind her, Rain says, What happens when you die?

Already? Alex thinks. She says, Our bodies go back into the earth.

When a mousie dies, where does it go?

Same as us. We all go back into the earth.

Rain holds something out. Alex shines the flashlight on it. A mouse. She grits her teeth and takes it from Rain's palm. Where did you find this? Alex asks. The mouse's front paws are folded together, body stiff.

Under my bed.

Dead?

Rain nods.

Alex says, Let's bury it.

Rain looks around at the snow. In the ground?

Yup. The body will decompose and rejoin the soil and come back as— Alex pauses. She sounds like Rose, all this woo-woo rebirth stuff.

Grass? Rain offers.

Grass, Alex agrees. She gets a shovel, and behind the shed, she scoops through the snow and chips at the ground until her arms hurt. She has Rain place the mouse into the shallow grave.

He says, Goodnight, Mousie.

Alex crouches and cups Rain's chin. Don't tell Maman you had the mouse in your pocket, okay?

Rain nods. He stands watch as Alex shovels dirt and snow over the body.

While they pile the first load of logs into the wheelbarrow, Rain says, You chopped the wood, and Maman lit the fire, and the smoke went outside and made clouds and turned into rain.

What's that?

And if Maman chops the wood, and you light the fire to make smoke to make clouds, that makes snow.

Alex pauses, a log in each hand: Has Rose mentioned a sibling to Rain? Does she want to name the next baby Snow? Alex is bewildered by her son, and not for the first time.

Rain clutches an armful of small branches, waiting for her. You don't like my stories?

I do, Alex says. Light flakes drift around them. And you can tell me more stories later. Right now, we've got to get this wood to the house, or we'll all be icicles in the morning.

Icicles, Rain repeats, and runs toward the cabin. Icicles icicles by morning we'll be icicles.

Rain loses steam after the second trip, and Alex makes the final through earnest, heavy snow. By the time she locks the wheelbarrow in the shed, the elements have reclaimed the mouse's grave. Her arms and hands and thumb, her legs, her back and belly ache and ache.

They wake to a blizzard so thick they can't see the shed or wood-line. Rose scrambles eggs and fries bacon. Alex reads last Sunday's paper, and Rain draws, and they eat in relative peace, Neuf meowing for scraps. Rose slips him some yolk, and Alex gets up to do the dishes.

Depositing the skillet in the sink, Rose whispers, You didn't set the traps.

Alex wants to say, Neither did you; instead she says, I'll do it later.

But Rain's clambering onto furniture and tugging at Alex's elbow, asking to be read to, or to play hide and seek, or to turn up the music and dance. Rose obliges him on this last one, cranking the volume and shimmying around the family room while Rain shuffles in a funny polka—*He has your moves*, Rose mouths—and no amount of cajoling gets Alex off the couch. Alex tries to read, tries to close her eyes, tries for a minute alone in the kitchen, but it's useless. She plays a game of Go Fish, and when the snow lulls right before dusk, she takes Rain out to play. He tromps around the yard, his shrieks cutting the quiet. A few minutes later, Rose joins them, and they watch Rain throw snow in the air.

Good thing we don't have neighbors, Alex says. Maybe this will tucker him out.

I used to wish for snow when I was a kid, Rose says.

And now you wish for palm trees? Alex asks.

No, Rose says. I don't miss L.A. at all.

Would it be so bad for him, as an only child?

He'll be lonely. I was.

Janna and James will have kids. He'll have cousins. My parents. Us.

Rain starts assembling a snow family like he does every storm, the smallest one taking shape, soon to be followed by two larger ones that Rose will help build, and a very small one for Neuf.

And when we die? Rose says. Her hair blows against her cheeks. Flecked with white, the red jumps even brighter than usual. Rose's hair was what caught Alex's eye the night they met.

Which won't be for a long time, Alex says.

That's probably what my parents said.

Alex looks at her feet, plunged in snow. There's no guarantee I can get pregnant.

Rose crosses her arms.

Can you imagine what the guys at work would say? Alex says.

Is that what you're worried about—the guys at work?

How will we pay the bills? It's not like I have maternity leave. And I can't exactly be using power tools—

They could switch you to the office for a little while. We have savings. Rose turns to Alex with the same look she leveled when she decided it was time they leave the city. All fierce fire—if Alex says no, she does so at her own peril. It doesn't leave much room for choice, but then, hasn't Rose's happiness always been Alex's first choice?

I don't know if I can do it, Alex says.

You could at least try. Rose holds Alex's eyes a moment longer.

Alex wants to reach for her, to say Yes, to say, Of course, darling, for you anything. But she thinks of her belly swelling, and her hips widening, and her breasts heavy with milk, she thinks of how tender and open Rose was after Rain's birth—a softness that Alex cherished, but cannot comprehend for her own body. Alex looks out over the wild white expanse of yard.

Rose walks to where Rain pats a ball of snow into semismoothness. She kneels and wipes Rain's face and asks him something—he nods—and then she begins the base of a big snowperson.

After dinner, Alex slips on her coat and says, I'm going downstairs.

Now? Rose asks. She sits on the couch with Rain curled in her lap. The fire is high and hot. A stockpile of candles and flashlights crowd the coffee table. Rain holds a copy of *The Tale of Johnny Town-Mouse*. Of all the books in the house.

I won't be long. The way the wind hurls through the trees, pelting the cabin with icy plinks, she's surprised the power's still on.

In the basement, she cranks the space heater and stands in front of it for a few minutes with her eyes closed. Then she goes to her workbench and unrolls the plans she's sketched for an addition. She's spoken to her parents about the cost of materials, and they've agreed; the cabin has been too tight for a while. A guest room, a study, a screened-in back porch —but Alex hasn't mentioned any of this to Rose. She'll have the old, mahogany crib in one of those rooms before Alex can even get the drywall up.

She re-rolls the plans, gets out the rocking horse she's

making for Rain. Upstairs, Rose's footsteps thump across the kitchen floor; cabinet doors open and close. Is she selfish, to consider saying no? Will she regret the word? Will Rain? She selects a piece of wood for the tail, flips on the bandsaw. Her fingers maneuver the wood into the blade. Her thumb is still sore from the other day, but she gets lost in the dance of carving, the push and pull, the agility.

She tries to picture guiding wood through the blurring metal with a pregnant belly—would her arms even be long enough? The image makes her laugh, and her hand lingers in place a second too long. She screams. Then the power snaps off, plunging the room into darkness.

The door at the top of the stairs flies open, and Rose descends with a flashlight, Rain close behind. She says, Are you— and then, Oh, bloody goodness.

Alex opens her mouth to say she's fine but only a low moan comes out.

Rose tucks the flashlight under her arm and squints in the dim light. Everything's still attached, Rose says. She unwinds her scarf, wraps it tight around Alex's hand. Blood seeps right through. Are you going to faint?

Is Ma dying? Rain asks.

She's not dying, Rose says. We need to get her upstairs. Can you carry the flashlight?

Upstairs, the fire blazes, far too warm. Emergency room? Alex gets out.

But Rose says, In this storm? steering her into the kitchen. She sits Alex down, lays newspaper on the table, unwraps the scarf. Rain scrabbles into his chair to watch Rose inspect the slice. I'm going to have to stitch you.

No-no-no-no-no, Alex says. We have to go to the emergency room.

We'd never make it, Rose says, filling the teakettle with water. To Rain, she says, Get Maman's kit from under the bathroom sink.

But— Alex squeaks. The pain and the heat press in on her.

I know what I'm doing, Rose says. Stay calm. She wets a paper towel and dabs away blood, bits of skin, the wound like a mouth screaming.

Maybe just bandage it, till tomorrow, Alex manages.

This sweater's done for, Rose says as she eases it over Alex's head, down off her arm. You're bleeding way too much. Rain carries in the kit, and Rose opens it, finds a bottle, shakes a pill into her palm. Swallow, she says, placing the pill in Alex's mouth, holding up a glass of water. Then she threads a needle.

Rain looks from Rose to Alex, his eyes welling.

Rose says, Let's wash our hands—I'm going to need your help. The kettle whistles, and Rose pours water into a bowl, dips the needle. Everything has to be very clean, she says, and Rain nods. Otherwise, Ma could get sick. Rose tells Alex to keep her arm vertical, but Alex can't, woozy from the pain and the pill seeping through her. Rose says, Rain, hold Ma's arm like this.

Bloody gauze, the smell of alcohol. The needle punctures the skin, and Alex flinches, biting her lip so hard she worries Rose'll have to stitch that next. She turns her focus to Rain, who watches Rose, rapt.

Rose says, See: make small, even stitches, pushing gently —skin is delicate.

Rain inches closer, and Alex notices how steady his small hands are, gripping her arm, not letting her wobble. Each time the needle pierces, she fights the urge to scream and to yank her hand away. More pills, she wants to say, but her tongue sticks in her mouth. She remembers Rose squatting, grinding her teeth during Rain's birth, the pale shock of her face as the midwife said, *Hospital. Now.* And how Rose refused until Alex and the midwife half-dragged her to the car. The slash across her belly afterward looked like she'd been sawed in half, but she never once complained that it hurt.

Now Rose angles the flashlight closer, ties a tiny knot and cuts the thread. See how brave Ma was? Just like you. Let's clean it, and then we'll wrap her.

Ma, Ma, look what Maman did, Rain says.

Alex doesn't want to, but Rain sounds so proud. In the web of her thumb, the stitches stick up like barbed wire or cactus spines. Blood marks fine lines like calligraphy on her skin.

Rain counts the tiny Xs. Five, he says.

They are, Alex thinks, perfect.

Rose takes Rain into the living room, and Alex hears her tucking him into the sleepaway, murmuring, Thank you for all your help, and Goodnight, and Yes, Ma will be fine. Alex holds her throbbing hand to her chest, thinks about what Rose is capable of—the strength in her delicacy—how perhaps the sturdiness Alex is so afraid of losing, Rose has had inside her all along.

With her good hand, Alex balls the gauze and newspaper, trashes it, picks up the needle by the bit of thread still attached, drops it in the bowl of water, packs up the kit. Rose comes back, says, How do you feel? and Alex says, Mutilated.

Are the pills working? They're expired.

Alex nods.

Time for sleep then.

They lie down next to Rain. Soon the sleepaway will be too small for this, and their power-out configuration will have to be readjusted.

I don't know— Alex says.

Shhh— Rose says and brings her face close to Alex's.

If I'll ever be able— a snap comes from the kitchen —to make you happy.

This house, all that's in it— Rose says. Another snap, this one accompanied by a squeak.

Is that the traps?

I set them while you were downstairs, Rose says. Why the Havaharts?

Moment of weakness, Alex says.

We should've got poison instead.

We're surrounded, aren't we.

It's a full-on family reunion, Rose says. Long-lost cousins, great aunts and uncles.

The stuff of nightmares, Alex says.

After a while Rose says, I am happy.

But this will make you happier, Alex says.

It's for Rain, Rose says. I mean it when I say I don't want him to be in this alone.

Alex says, We'll need more space.

Rose says, Especially with all these mice.

Ma, Rain says, squirming under the blankets. Ma.

Let her sleep, Rose says from the kitchen.

I'm awake, Alex says.

Rain burrows in. He says, Will you read to me? He holds the copy of *Johnny Town-Mouse.*

Be careful, Rose says. Ma's hand is sore.

It hurts, Ma? Rain asks.

Alex holds her bandaged hand over the blankets. Blood spots a few places. A little, Alex says, though it throbs like a split-open heart. Is there coffee?

Almost. Rose comes in, pointing toward the tin pot steaming on the woodstove. She hands Alex a sweater and long johns, says, The kitchen's freezing.

Can we go outside? Rain asks.

Go wash up in the bucket in the bathroom, okay? Rose says, lowering her voice: We have to deal with the mice.

What are we going to do with them? Alex asks.

Rose shrugs, looks toward the back door.

We can't just throw them in the snow, Alex says.

I'm going to compost them, Rose says.

That's repulsive.

I read about it in that homesteading book. The heat—

We put the compost on our garden.

The heat neutralizes the bacteria. You remember that couple with the cow.

I remember. Alex says, trying to push the image away. I wish you hadn't told me.

You asked.

Mamas? Rain yells. Mousie—

Alex says, I'll go.

In the bathroom, Rain leans over the bucket, where a mouse floats, edged against the skin of ice atop the water.

Did you touch it? Alex asks.

Rain shakes his head, says, All the mousies are dying.

Mice, Alex says, squatting down to eye level with Rain. And there will be more mice. I promise. She wraps the mouse in a rag, leaves the water to use in the toilet tank.

In the kitchen, Rose stares out the window. There are a lot of mice, she says. Neuf sits on the table, licking his chops.

Dead? Rain asks.

Dead, Alex says, swatting Neuf with the flat of her hand.

He circles around the three of them, all impatience. We need a bucket.

We have to bury them, Rain says. Ma knows a place.

Alex avoids Rose's eyes, and shoos Neuf outside, grabbing the ash bucket by the back door, happy to be no longer holding the mouse in its shroud.

Rose sucks in a big breath and opens the cabinet beneath the sink. Alex has never seen anything like it: a tidy row of carnage.

What's carnage? Rain asks.

It means there are a lot of dead things, Rose says, calmly lifting a mouse by the metal jaws that clamp its neck, releasing it into the bucket.

Rain watches each body fall. Can I touch? he asks.

No, Rose says. In the other cabinets, more bodies wait. Finished with those, Rose leans back on her heels and sighs. The Havaharts are in the pantry.

There is a mouse in both traps. We've caught ourselves a youngster and a plumpster, Alex says.

Rose looks at the bigger one, says, Maybe it's pregnant.

Rain crowds Alex's arm, looking into the traps, says, Which one's gonna have babies?

Rose says, What should we do?

Keep them? Rain suggests.

Alex looks at her son and pictures an endless line of mice, generation after generation, taking over the cabin. She can't help but laugh.

The storm has moved on, leaving the sky a high, dull gray. Alex holds Rain's hand. Rose carries the bucket of bodies and the Havaharts. In one smooth arc of her arm, she dumps the corpses into the compost, says, From where you came, you shall return.

Rain echoes her.

The first Havahart releases its tiny captive without trouble, but the second trap's door refuses to budge. I need your help, Rose says. The fat brown body trembles.

Johnny Town-Mouse—please can we keep him? Rain asks.

No, Rose says at the same time that Alex says, Her. Alex uses her good hand to fiddle with the jammed mechanism.

Rain says, Please?

She's wild. She doesn't belong in a cage, Rose says.

That's a cage, Rain says.

Only so we can get her outside, Rose says. Rain's lower lip quivers, and Rose leads him away, saying, Let's make angels. Rose's hair pops against the snow like bittersweet.

Eventually, Alex breaks the door off the trap. The mouse curls tight toward the back. All right, Mama—good luck, Alex says, tilting the cage, and the mouse falls out, tunnels away.

Rose and Rain lay in the snow, arms and legs pumping. Alex drops next to Rose and moves her legs and good arm, relishing the tickle of powder that swirls and settles over her. Rain jumps up, runs toward yesterday's snow family, now half-buried.

Alex turns to Rose, cheek pressed against the cold, and says, I drew plans for an addition.

Rose sits up, and Alex does, too. They watch Rain circling the snow-family.

A three-season porch, a playroom—another bedroom.

Rose's eyes glisten, and Alex understands what she should have long ago: This was not a battle Rose waged to win. It is a room only Alex can build.

Rain yells, C'mon, Mamas. Look at all this snow. We gotta make more.

Slice

Sebastian's knock broke my reverie. I'd been fastening the collar piece to the bodice and a straight pin pierced the pad of my index finger. Blood welled. I sucked away the drop, careful not to stain the silk.

It's open, I said.

The door's rusty hinges scraped, and Sebastian came in holding a paper bag from the hardware store. He gave the mannequin a wide berth and kissed me hello. Straight from work, he smelled of ink and screen-press steam.

I didn't expect you so early, I said.

Thought I'd fix that screen, he said. Keep the mosquitoes out. From the bag, he pulled a flathead screwdriver, some rubber cording, a tool that looked like a small pizza cutter, and a jar of miso paste.

Is miso the secret ingredient?

That, he said, is for dinner. Those eggplants are about to go limp.

Feel this fabric, I said. Smooth as water. Near impossible to work with, but gorgeous, huh?

Sebastian rubbed the silk between his fingers. He eyed me and smiled, revealing his wolfish, crooked teeth.

I said, Don't say it.

Why not? he said, untucking my T-shirt and stroking my belly. It's true.

His fingers fumbled with the button of my jeans, and we leaned into that rip current between us. I let him unzip me, but then stepped away, said, Don't tease. I can't stop now.

Neither can I, he said, but I intercepted his hand, held it.

Finally got my Singer back, I said, gesturing as if he might have missed the gleaming black hulk dominating the table. An inheritance from my grandmother, with its worn gold decals and engraved silver-plate.

Lucky it was still there, Sebastian said.

I'm not sure the pawnshop turns a lively trade in sewing machines, I said. I'd hocked it for the deposit on my apartment, trusting just that. My receptionist paychecks never added up to enough, but the first half of the commission for this dress—from a friend of a friend of an old friend, an indie actress wanting something wildly unique for an award dinner—finally brought it home.

Sebastian circled the mannequin, like a dog sniffing a stranger. The chest bristled with straight pins. Did this big voodoo doll come from the pawnshop, too?

From that junk shop on Market.

You sleep with it in here?

It doesn't even have a head.

Exactly, Sebastian said. All it needs is a horse.

I cover it before bed, I said. To protect the fabric. You won't even know it's here. I eased a pin out, adjusted the collar and bodice, pushed the pin back in. The pieces bunched, the silk slippery and my fingers tired.

Sebastian said, I'll do the screen down in the yard. Do you think you'll work all night?

I shook my head.

This won't take me long, Sebastian said.

He started unscrewing the screen from the frame. His Dickies, a pair I hadn't seen before, were hemmed unevenly. Marie's handiwork, and most likely I'd find the bottom thread loopy and snarled when I let them out to fix. I'm sure Marie possessed many fine traits—Sebastian had wanted to marry her, after all—but tailoring was not among them.

I repositioned the collar, pausing between each pin to watch Sebastian wrestle with the frame, swearing and wiping his hands, until he managed to dislodge it. With the screen gone, the back door gaped, the sunset beyond it glowing molten pink as a cactus flower.

It's sweltering in here, Sebastian said. He faced me, balancing the screen on his foot. All these lights lit up like you're trying to land a plane.

Or do piecework, I said. Truth was, I liked the bright heat that accompanied a project—it meant I was plunged into the promise of turning cloth into costume, the warmth of creating a new skin.

'd taken the bus down to Manhattan to meet the actress—Chloe—and to measure her, talk styles, materials, fit, color. After we covered the basics, Chloe launched into a story about the Lady of the Lake and her enchantment of Merlin by his own magic. We sat in her living room in Gramercy, a spacious square furnished with two white linen couches and nothing else, and I watched her slender, tapered fingers illustrate energetic connection, the spell love casts, the power of water, how one must surrender to fate even if it means destruction.

So, you want the dress to look like you've stepped from a mythic lake, I said.

Sort of, Chloe said. I think I know exactly what I need to show you.

We walked over to the Union Square Farmers' Market, and she waved and chatted with the people in the stalls until we got to the right booth. She held up a skinny, deep-purple eggplant topped by a dark, spiky cap.

She said, This is how I want the dress to look.

I took the eggplant from her, examined it, said, This I can do. She filled a paper bag and sent me home.

Since then, my apartment has overflowed with Japanese eggplant. Sebastian brought recipes, and replacements from his father's garden and the farm stand up the road. He fashioned wire contraptions to stand them up, turning my windowsill into an eggplant catwalk.

They're the Bond Girl of vegetables, Sebastian said the night I basted the drop-waist bodice to the skirt. We'd just finished a toaster-oven rendition of eggplant parm—no easy feat in my two-burner-hotplate and dorm-fridge kitchen—and knelt, soaping dishes in the clawfoot bathtub, the apartment's only luxury, even if it doubled as sink.

I don't get it, I said.

Beautiful to look at, he said. But kind of bland.

I've never seen a Bond movie, I said.

You're kidding. How did I not know this?

Until the dress subsumed me, we'd spent most of our evenings on the futon watching foreign films (my choice) and horror movies (his) on the TV he'd brought over. He wasn't using it; his parents owned a bigger one with a better screen.

Dishes dripping in the makeshift drying rack, Sebastian said, You deserve a treat. How about we go to the diner?

Or we could take a bath, I said. The idea of getting in the car, and sitting under the fluorescents, vinyl sticking to my thighs, made me tired.

Too warm for that, Sebastian said. And since when do you turn down pie?

I had a thing for the diner's lemon meringue—the waitress made it; she made all the pies. She flirted with Sebastian and had once said to me, when Sebastian was in the bathroom, *If he's not the cherry on top.* By her sharp, over-blushed cheekbones and perfect posture, I could tell she had once been beautiful.

She flashed her fuchsia grin as we slid into our usual booth, and brought our pie and coffees. Out of nowhere, Sebastian said, We're celebrating, and the waitress beamed, said, Let me see the ring.

Sebastian's face went red.

I placed both hands flat on the Formica, said, No ring.

For a moment, we all focused on the whipped peaks of the pie.

I just hit a milestone on a big project, I said, picturing the purple-black silk rippling like a phantom. We're celebrating that.

The waitress pursed her lips, said, That's worthy of a second slice. On me.

There had been a ring. Not mine. Marie's. I'd seen it: an antique passed down through several generations of Sebastian's grandmothers, half-carat in an ornate bezel setting, bestowed upon Marie years ago and returned last fall, right around the time I cut my losses in the city and hauled my paltry belongings to Northampton.

I scooped up a bite of pie. The lemon tasted sharp. Fatigue pressed behind my eyes. Can we take this home? I asked, setting down my spoon.

In the car, Sebastian said, How awkward. He shifted and then pressed my thigh. Sorry.

It's not your fault, I said. She's a lonely old romantic. I said it to comfort him, but in the silence that followed, I wondered if I wasn't the one who needed it.

S ebastian had booked the trip to Newport a few months earlier, when I had no reason to foresee a commission like the dress. Now those five vacation days stood, non-refundable, between me and getting the dress to Chloe on time.

I hustled to get the major seams stitched, but the hems and lining and beading and buttons—details that transformed a gown from pretty to luxe—loomed.

Two nights before leaving, Sebastian showed up, whistling, and looked over the dress. He said, An eggplant fit for a queen.

Hardly, I said. It's like your Bond Girls. Without depth.

But stunning, he said. You could wear it out right now.

The dress eddied around the mannequin. I thought of what Chloe had told me about the Lady of the Lake emerging from the mist to bestow *Excalibur* upon Arthur. It wasn't royalty I wanted to capture, but something else, something richer.

It has to be more than stunning, I said.

You're awfully hard on yourself, Sebastian said.

I don't think you understand what this dress means, I said.

Maybe I don't, he said. But I think you're burning out.

We're going on vacation—time I can't afford to take— and I need to get this to a point where I can leave. I popped open my sewing kit, found the needle I needed, threaded it. I said, I have to baste the lining tonight.

Sebastian said, Do you mind if I watch something?

Maybe I should have said No, I need to concentrate. Instead I said, As long as you keep the sound low.

I laid out the lining, began tacking. That part was quick —Sebastian was only halfway through *The Shining* when I finished—so I turned on the sewing machine, set in the permanent stitches. Sebastian moved closer to the TV, but didn't turn the volume up. As I sailed over the seams, I regretted being sharp with him. Here he was, cooking me dinner every night, treating me to a vacation, complimenting my creations. No one had ever taken such good care of me.

I finished the lining, and thought about setting it in, but decided to wait. It was almost midnight. I tugged the pull chain on my work lamp, and the floor lamp I'd scavenged street-side, switched on the window fan. I got two popsicles from the freezer and joined Sebastian on the futon. He sat flipping through a book on design drawing techniques.

I'm excited about our vacation, I said.

He closed the book, said, How would you feel about getting out of this place?

This place? I asked. You mean, town?

I mean— He traced his finger along the cover's inlay and looked around the apartment.

Move in together? I asked. I pointed at his popsicle with mine. Better eat that before it melts.

You think it's too soon? he asked.

I think it's impossible to get a red stain out, I said.

He downed his popsicle in three bites, and worried the wooden stick between his fingers. I'm always here, he said, and I thought—it'd be nice to—share a bigger space.

I scanned my meager belongings: a few sketches taped to the wall over the table, the mannequin covered for the night, two mismatched kitchen chairs, books in tall stacks, Tupperware filled with fabric and supplies, the sewing machine. Easy to box up, to carry elsewhere. Sebastian had a point—the place was tight with the two of us, never meant to hold more than one person. A huge piece of me tugged toward Sebastian's offer, but another part pulled toward the anchor I'd let down in this apartment, the first I'd lived in alone, the first that felt like home.

Let me think on it, I said.

It's big, I know.

Will there be a sewing room?

We can probably finagle that, he said. He rubbed my back.

Mmm, I said, leaning into his hands. I'm very tempted.

n the morning, when I got to work, I called Chloe with an update. I liked the salon best the hour I spent there alone, brewing coffee, running over the appointment book, before the hair dryers and chatter crowded the high-ceilinged room. Chloe asked if I'd received the book she'd mailed, a tome of Arthurian legends. I had, I told her, and planned on bringing it to Newport, to read on the beach.

Things are well, then, with your beau? she asked.

He asked me to move in with him, I said.

That's huge, Chloe said. How long have you been together?

Eight months, I said. I haven't given him an answer.

The sun lifted from behind the buildings across the street and flooded the salon, transforming the dust around the front desk into a million sparkling pinpricks, a luminosity like being plunged into a lake of light. So many mornings this curious moment surrounded me like a blessing from ghosts I couldn't shake free.

Why not? she asked. Not that you need to answer *me*.

It's hope, I guess.

Hope is the thing stopping you?

Hope's gotten me into a lot of trouble.

I can tell you live heart-forward, she said. I can tell you're brave.

Brave is putting it kindly, I said. What did Chloe know? We'd met once, emailed and talked on the phone a half-dozen times.

Read the book, she said. I cannot wait to see this marvel of a dress.

The sun climbed out of the window, and the glimmering mirage snapped back to invisibility.

t took some digging to find my bathing suit—tucked in a
side pocket of a suitcase I'd dragged from one coast to the
other and back again—a bikini, printed like a red bandana,
those triangles not looking big enough to cover much of anything. If I'd had any extra money, I'd have gone and pur-
chased something more reasonable, but in my overnight bag
it went, along with some old sundresses and sunscreen, and
the book from Chloe.

Sebastian knocked at nine the next morning, offered to
take my bags down.

Bag, I said. I'll manage. Come inside for a minute. I
poured coffee into travel mugs, handed him his and said, My
answer is yes.

Hesitation flickered across his face, almost like he didn't
remember the question, but he recovered and kissed me and
said, A grand new palace for my sexy seamstress, and kissed
me again.

The coffee got cold.

Once on the highway, Sebastian pulled a cassette tape
from his shirt pocket. Made this for you, he said, popping it
into the deck. Weezer sheared through the speakers: *Let's go
away for a while, you and I, to a strange and distant land, where
they speak no word of truth—*

Sebastian rubbed my thigh, cast his eyes over at me until
I worried he'd drive into a guardrail. I propped my bare feet
on the dash, rolled down the window, and let the wind knot
my hair. Some of the songs we sang along to, but for entire
stretches we watched the trees and highway dividers and
shopping malls and other cars reel past, silence easy between us. We crossed the Rhode Island state line and wound
the narrow roads down into Newport. Sebastian parked in
front of a bed and breakfast, pink with white trim, like a big
cake or a dress Marie Antoinette might've worn. Unlike anything I'd ever stayed in.

Here we are, he said.

Adorable, I said.

Inside, Sebastian gave his name. The owner fluttered
around behind her big wooden desk, grabbed a key, flipped
some pages in a book, and said to me, You must be Marie.

The key dangled from her hand by a velvet ribbon, one
of those cast-iron barrel affairs. It had to be a reproduction.

I realized she was holding it out to us. Sebastian had his hands jammed in his pockets.

Emmeline, I said, accepting the key with a forced smile.

The owner smiled back and with a curious glance in Sebastian's direction, said, Must've written it down wrong. I *am* getting to be a lady of a certain age. Come, come.

I followed them up a curving, grand staircase, down a hallway. She pushed open a heavy mahogany door, and we stepped into a big room with a canopy bed decked out in white eyelet and a mountain of frilled pillows. She showed us the complimentary champagne and how to work the TV, and I half-listened, paying more attention to the red velvet chairs flanking the bay window, the cross-stitch sampler on the wall: *Knowledge is knowing a tomato is a fruit. Wisdom is not putting it in a fruit salad.* I wanted her to leave, but when she did, I clutched my overnight bag, not knowing if it would be worse to get back in the car and drive home or to say, Let's go down to the shore. Either way, something inside me had split, and I wondered how fast I could mend the tear, if it were worth salvaging.

Sebastian concentrated all his focus on unlacing his Chuck Taylors. I can explain, he finally started, but a knock on the door interrupted, and he said, Come in.

The owner bustled by with a tray of chocolate-dipped strawberries, a bottle of sparkling water. Lovebird special, she chirped, setting it on the trunk by the foot of the bed. Compliments of the house.

I set down my bag, said, You're too kind.

Ring if you need anything. She pointed to the brass bell on the dresser before exiting.

Explain what, exactly? I asked.

Sebastian looked out the window, hands clasped in his lap like he was praying. He curled his toes on the plush carpet.

I could be home, I said. Working on my dress.

I'm so tired of that dress, he said. It's not even yours.

That's sweet, I said. Coming from the person taking me on his ex-fiancée's vacation. Did you make that tape for her, too?

It's not what you think, Sebastian said.

Then why did that woman call me Marie? All I could

think of was hand-me-downs—the waists I'd let out, the sleeves I'd removed, the pleats I'd folded to conceal stains— how good I was at beautifying what others had cast off. Most of my favorite clothing, the dresses I'd packed, had once belonged to others.

Sebastian hesitated. She asked for both of our names when I made the reservation. I must've given her the wrong one.

An honest mistake, maybe. How many years had he been giving Marie's name—and mine only a few months. So here we were, together in a strange room, neither of us quite willing to leave.

I feel like an asshole, he said. Forgive me? He held out his hand.

Past him, and the lace curtains framing the bay window, lay sand dunes sloping down to the ocean, topped by a broad wash of turquoise. Like a postcard—finally, something worth writing home about. I pressed the heel of my hand against my breastbone, trying to ease the strain, determined not to let it rip. Then I stooped and pushed past the book in my bag, searching for my suit.

I said, Give me a minute to change, and then let's go.

Sebastian looked at his bare feet. Where?

To the beach, I said. A little saltwater would do us good.

Our last night in Newport, I dragged Sebastian to the arcade where we played Skee-Ball until tickets over-flowed from our pockets, and the little kids around us cheered Sebastian's streak of 50s. We redeemed the tick-ets for a human-sized hot-pink elephant, which accompa-nied us to the ice cream parlor for cones.

On our way back to the B & B, I said, Let's go down to the water.

Sebastian said, Now? The elephant practically glowed in the dark.

I wanted to put my feet in the water one last time, squish the sand between my toes. Sebastian watched as I ran into the waves, getting the hem of my dress wet. I hollered, Come in, come in, but he didn't. The cold curled around my calves, and I didn't notice I'd cut myself until I made my way back to Sebastian, wincing at the sand grinding into my heel.

You're bleeding a lot, Sebastian said.

With all the sand stuck to my foot, and no light to see by, neither of us could assess the depth or size of the wound. Elephant under one arm, supporting me with the other, Sebastian hobbled us back, and at the threshold, he dropped the elephant and scooped me up. Can't have you bleeding on the carpet, he said. I hear red stains last forever.

He carried me into the bathroom, sat me on the edge of the tub, and washed my foot. Blood and sand swirled down the drain.

He said, It's deep. I think stitches.

Not without insurance, I said. A Band-Aid will have to do.

The gash needed more than a Band-Aid, but I wouldn't budge. Sebastian said he'd pay for it, but after several refusals, he went for butterfly bandages, gauze and medical tape, iodine, a bottle of ibuprofen.

The next morning, I couldn't put pressure on my foot, and Sebastian loaded the car and checked out while I sat by the window, looking at the ocean, wishing I could run down again and say goodbye. I'd gathered a jam jar full of rocks and shells and sand, but it wasn't till we were halfway home that I realized I'd forgotten it on the dresser.

Climbing three flights of stairs was rough, but Sebastian got me into my apartment, and settled, offered to stay. I'm going to work, I told him, so he kissed me goodbye. I turned on all the lights. I took the dress off the mannequin and draped it over my lap, propped my foot up, uncapped the dish of seed beads. All night, I embroidered the collar. Lost in the monotony, I didn't recognize dawn. When my alarm went off, I called in sick, made coffee. All morning and afternoon, I stitched those beads. By sunset, the collar looked like a mussel shell, drenched in the last rays of daylight.

The next night, when Sebastian stopped by, I was beading down the shoulders and back for the spiky cap effect. He pointed to two wrinkled eggplants, said,

I suppose I'll cook those for you—they're on their last legs.

I may never eat eggplant again, I said.

Do you think you'll get more work from this? Sebastian asked. Thread bunched around a bead, and I bent to examine it, reached for the scissors. Before I could answer, he said, That elephant is truly ridiculous.

Next dress I make, I said, will be for that elephant.

Between the elephant or the mannequin, I don't know what's freakier.

All those horror movies are getting to you.

If this dress takes off, you could be huge, Sebastian said.

I don't want to be huge, I said. How many times I'd heard that. How tired I was of the inherent expectation.

He smoothed his hands over his thighs, said, What do you want then?

I took one of his hands in mine. Looked at the tattoo on his wrist: *L'amour est mort*, in curving script. I'd once joked I had a similar tattoo—*L'amour est une illusion*—inked on my heart. You, I said. I want to live in this little town with you.

Sebastian squeezed my hand. That could change.

Believe me, I said. I'm not going anywhere.

He looked away from me then, out the window, though it was dark. He said, I'm going to go after dinner. You have a lot of work.

I said, Stay, watch a movie.

No, he said. I don't want to distract you.

⁂

Most days, Sebastian visited on my lunch break, and we drank coffee at the metal tables outside the bakery next door. And maybe if I hadn't been consumed with finishing the dress, I would have worried when he didn't show up all week. The one time he called, he said, I don't want to stress you out. I said, You're not, but I didn't push. Hours slipped through my hands. Then, the afternoon I began the buttons—the fussiest detail, put off till last—he called and said, Can I come over? and I said, Of course, but I have to finish the buttons tonight, and he said, I won't stay. What time? and I said, Seven. We hung up, and I stared at my phone, trying to remember when we'd last made such specific plans for no reason.

Buttons involve persnickety, incremental measurements, and I'd stuck half the two hundred straight pins marking the placements when Sebastian knocked. I said, It's open.

He came in, and he did not kiss me but sat down at the table and rushed out, I have something to tell you.

What? I stabbed a pin into the tomato-shaped pincushion he'd given me.

He picked up a button and pressed it between his thumb and finger.

I said, Do I have to guess?

He said, Marie—

Again?

She called. And—we've been talking.

My chest tightened. In my hands, the tomato looked like a barbed heart.

She says she made a mistake. She wants to—start over.

I squeezed the pincushion. Pins bit into my palm, my fingers. And you do, too, I said, the words barely escaping.

Will you look at me, he said.

When I did, he tried to loosen my grip on the pincushion, but I held fast.

I've loved her since I was fifteen. I never stopped.

The tightness spread up my throat, into my jaw. What about us?

This isn't a decision I ever wanted to make, he said. I don't want to hurt you—

But you will anyway. The pain in my hands, in my chest, flared.

From his pocket, he produced a cassette and set it on the table. I'm so sorry.

I don't want that, I said.

I made it for you. It's yours.

After he left, I smashed the tape with the heavy handle of my shears, unspooled the ribbon, and snipped it to pieces. None of it, I thought—not the eggplant dishes, not the lemon meringue pie, not the big bed in Newport, not the patched screen—had ever been mine.

C hloe answered the door, said, Darling, you've arrived, and with a sweep of her eyes, continued, Are you limping?

A little, I said. Nothing major.

I hope you took a cab, she said, leading me down the hallway to her bedroom where she settled onto an ottoman. I've been eagerly awaiting this unveiling.

I opened the dress box and unfolded the dress.

Chloe gave a little gasp and covered her mouth.

I'll wait in the kitchen while you try it, I said. Do you mind if I grab some water?

On her countertop were wooden bowls of vegetables: green beans, bell peppers, cucumber, zucchini, beets, and, of course, eggplant. On the wall over the butcher's block hung a framed charcoal drawing I hadn't noticed last time: a sword floating over a lake. *Excalibur*, I figured, studying the swirling currents. That was the one legend I'd had time to read. I wondered, now, what it felt like to hold invincibility in your hands. Chloe bustled in with the dress.

Is something wrong? I asked. I reached for my bag—I'd brought everything necessary for an alteration.

Not that, she said. But I have a favor. Will you put it on? Me?

I want an objective view. We're about the same size.

I—

Pretty please, she said, thrusting the dress at me.

In her dressing room, I shed my cotton shift, slipped into the cool length of silk. The collar, the shoulders, weighed on me like a yoke. The buttons took forever and, once done up, made it hard to breathe. Chloe had left a pair of heels, and I stepped into them, looked in the three-way mirror. The dress shone like water in moonlight, a sinuous, bruisy ripple.

When I went into the kitchen, Chloe squealed. You're a genius, she said.

I ate a lot of eggplant to get this just so, I said.

Method-sewing, she said.

I might've laughed if the dress didn't threaten to rip.

After I'd hung the dress in her closet and rejoined her in the kitchen, she pointed to a flat, wrapped box on the table.

A token, she said.

A pair of antique embroidery scissors, Gothic cast-brass handle and straight steel blades; they looked like a miniature sword. This is too much, I said.

She flourished her hand, said, The moment I saw them, I knew they belonged to you.

Through her open window, strains of the city drifted in: snippets of conversation and laughter, a long siren, a jackhammer. A wave of nostalgia washed over me and curled back. From the way Chloe stared at me, I worried she might ask a question I didn't want to answer.

I said, I'll miss my bus if I don't hurry.

Chloe insisted on hailing a cab, following me downstairs and stepping into the street, her arm high. Once I climbed in, she leaned through my window.

I said, Thank you.

She pressed my hand, searching my face, and said, Till next time, Emmeline. She gave the driver cash and waved from the curb.

It was rush hour, and the cab crept across town. The sun edged into the skyline, burning as pink as blistered skin. I opened the box and lifted the scissors, surprised by their heft. The taxi turned right, leaving behind the traffic to speed north. I slid my thumb and forefinger through the eye rings and watched the blades glimmer as they sliced the light.

Abandon

Calla opened her eyes, and there was Audrey. The overhead fluorescents glared. Audrey pressed the nurse call button. The nurse came in, and Audrey said, She won't stop blinking.

The nurse studied Calla, adjusted something on the tube snaking into the back of her hand. He said, How do you feel?

He had mismatched eyes, one blue and one brown. Calla tried to make sense of this. She tried to make sense of the bright light and aura of pressure around her head, the dull line of pain drawn across her abdomen.

Thirsty, she said.

The room swayed. Audrey and the nurse waved like seaweed. They talked, and the doctor came, and Calla tried to hear what they were saying. All she heard were echoes. She closed her eyes.

When Calla woke again, Audrey was sitting by the bed.

What are you doing here? Calla said.

Audrey pulled the chair closer, rested her elbows next to Calla's legs. Do you remember what happened?

We were on our way to a housewarming. There'd been an accident—the baby—

Audrey shook her head, not looking at Calla.

I lost the baby, Calla said. The words were unreal. Where's Gabriel?

Apparently he told the doctors he couldn't deal, Audrey said.

I need to call him, Calla said, propping herself up.

He's not answering his phone. Audrey stood, hovering in front of Calla, hand on her arm.

He'll answer if it's me, Calla said. Something rippled behind the blankness. To have her whole life torn away, without a moment's notice. She should be used to it by now, but she never was.

My name's still on your emergency contact card, Audrey said.

How long have you been here?

Four days.

Was I in a coma?

You were unconscious, and then medicated.

We were on our way to a party.

I didn't even know you were pregnant, Audrey said.

I was waiting till I passed twelve weeks. Then things got crazy.

And Gabriel?

I was going to call you. But you know—

I know, Audrey said, lifting her bag. You fall in love and lose sight of everything—

Are you angry?

A little. But I didn't call, either.

What do you mean? Calla gathered the blanket up to her chest.

I'll tell you later. Visiting hours are over. I need to go.

Back to New York?

I'm staying in your apartment.

When can I go home?

In a few days, I think.

alla lay awake a long time. Two nurses came to check on her, neither the one with the mismatched eyes. The second lifted the sheets and said, I'll just clean you up.

It took Calla a moment to understand. She was bleeding. She said, I lost the baby.

The nurse stopped, sponge in hand. Yes, dear. You did.

Looking down the length of her body, Calla saw a bandage over her abdomen. What's that?

The nurse eased up the tape, peeled back the gauze. Beneath was a raw slash, from her right hipbone diagonal down to her pubic bone, sutured shut.

Don't touch it, the nurse said.

Did they cut the baby out of me?

There was glass wedged beneath your seatbelt. It sliced you pretty deep.

The vase of flowers she held on her lap would have shattered, of course. But the wound looked like the baby had ripped through her.

Don't cry, dear. Take your pills—you need to rest.

The nurse rinsed the wound with saline, rebandaged her. She pulled the covers up and asked if Calla wanted another blanket. Once she was alone, Calla slipped her hand beneath the sheet, felt the blood coming from between her legs. It was warm. She kept her hand there, feeling the liquid drip from her. Then she brought her fingers to her mouth and tasted the blood. Salty and metallic. This is my baby, she thought.

Audrey brought Calla home to an immaculate apartment. Did you polish the floors? Calla asked.

Audrey shuffled her into the bedroom. The bed was made, and there was a stack of books and magazines on the nightstand. I tidied up a bit, Audrey said. I thought you'd appreciate coming home to a clean house.

In front of the closet sat two black garbage bags. Calla said, What's this?

Gabriel's clothes. I thought I'd save you the trouble.

You went through my stuff?

We can talk about it later. Get into bed. I'll bring you some water.

Calla did as she was told. She couldn't start an argument on painkillers. Her words formed too slowly. When do you go back? Calla asked. Ruth must be anxious.

I'm not, Audrey said.

You're not— anxious?

Going back to the city, Audrey said. I'm staying here.

In Northampton?

Audrey looked at the floor. Ruth left me for another woman. I lost my job. I got an eviction notice the morning the hospital called—it seemed, I don't know, like destiny.

Calla closed her eyes. Since when do you believe in destiny?

I thought you'd understand. That you'd be excited I'm here.

All she wanted was to be alone. But she would need groceries and to get to doctors' appointments. Who else but Audrey? I'm sorry about Ruth, Calla said.

I should have seen it coming.

They were quiet for a while. Audrey sat on the bed next to Calla, and Calla tried to smile.

It'll be like Brooklyn, living together, Audrey said. I've missed you.

Calla said, Where's that stuff for my cut?

Audrey dug through the bag of medicines. She pulled out a tube, squeezed ointment onto her finger.

Calla said, I'll do it. Beneath the scar, which flamed and sputtered with pain, Calla felt a tap-tap, like when the baby had kicked.

Audrey lingered while Calla lifted her shirt and undid the bandage.

I'm fine, Calla said. They showed me what to do.

Your hands are clean? Audrey asked. She stood back a little, her fingers knotted together.

Calla dabbed the ointment on, tried not to show how squeamish it made her. I'm fine, Audrey. I'm tired.

If you need me—

You'll be here. Got it.

Calla redressed the wound. It throbbed and then settled. She lay staring out the window at the bare branches of the neighbor's maple, scraping like fingers against the washed-out sky.

Audrey got a job at an animal shelter in Springfield, but finding an apartment didn't happen. She stayed on Calla's couch, did the dishes, cleaned the bathroom, dusted, and vacuumed until Calla told her to quit it.

As soon as she could, Calla went back to work at The Green Bean. They gave her short shifts—early morning, after lunch. She needed money, but her body wasn't quite up to earning it.

One morning, she brought a cup of coffee to table twelve. Are you ready? she asked.

The man looked up at her. He had one blue eye and one brown. Hi, he said.

Hi, Calla said. Her scar pulsed. The stitches were gone, but it was still an angry pink welt, sore to the touch. It also, Calla now understood, had a mind of its own. It reacted to things—with a tightening or a prickle or an itch. Sometimes it seemed to be singing.

How are you?

Fine, Calla said.

You don't remember me, do you.

Should I? Calla said.

The man laughed. Maybe not. Dylan. One of your nurses at Cooley.

Oh, Calla said. Of course—the mismatched eyes— Sorry, usually I have a better memory.

He smiled, and the scar pattered. He ordered breakfast and ate, and every time Calla looked over at his table, he was watching her. When she refilled his coffee, he said, Weather's been nice lately. Looks like winter might finally let go.

She thought for a minute that maybe he was right. On his way out, he winked at her—blue eye. She turned away, dizzy, pressing her hand over the scar.

Don't you think it's time to get rid of this stuff? Audrey asked, poking her bare foot into the trash bags of Gabriel's clothes that remained in front of the closet.

Calla put down the book she was reading. No, she said. For the thousandth time, no.

Have you tried calling him?

He'll come when he's ready. I don't see why it bothers you so much, Calla said.

Because it's obvious he's not worth a dime.

It's 'not worth a damn.'

Whatever. He's not worth anything. Aren't you angry?

What good will it do me to get angry? Can we stop talking about this? Whenever Gabriel's name came up, which was often with Audrey, the scar grew taut, like it was coiling, ready to strike.

Would you take him back?

I don't know.

Are you kidding me? That's the stupidest thing I've ever heard.

No wonder Ruth left you.

That's a shitty thing to say.

You just called me stupid, Calla said.

I didn't mean it, Audrey said. I just hate seeing you like this.

Like what?

Moping around.

Nobody's moping. I'm supposed to take it easy. In case you forgot—

I haven't forgotten.

He asked me to marry him.

He did?

When we found out I was pregnant.

Were you in love with him?

What kind of question is that?

I'll bring the clothes to Goodwill.

Forget about the clothes.

Audrey sat down on the floor. With some difficulty, she pulled her legs into a misshapen pretzel. She placed her hands on her knees. I'm going to take up meditation.

Now?

Not this minute. But LuLu was talking about it today. How much it helps her. Maybe you should try it, too.

Calla sighed. The last thing she wanted to do was sit still with her thoughts. She rubbed her thumb along the spine of her book. You've been talking about LuLu an awful lot.

Audrey's cheeks splotched red, and she brought her hands to her face as though to blot the color away. The animals adore her. And she's gorgeous. Drop-dead.

Straight, Calla said.

Audrey shrugged. I haven't figured it out. She hasn't mentioned any significant others.

Be careful, Calla said.

Always, Audrey said.

Never, Calla replied, picking up her book.

It was an old joke, but neither laughed.

The scar looked like a snake, the way its triangular tip rested atop her hipbone, a finer scar etched out like a tongue. Its pinkness did not lessen. The doctor told Calla it might not fade; on fair skin, scars often remained pronounced.

Calla didn't tell the doctor the scar kept her awake at night, that it had its own pulse. Nor did she tell the doctor that every time the nurse with mismatched eyes came into The Green Bean for breakfast, the scar set to humming.

Wordless, tuneless—a strange vibration, if pleasant.

Calla and Audrey took to walking. After dinner, they ambled through town, sometimes for hours, as the trees frilled out and tulips unfurled their petals. The scent of cut grass and cow manure hung heavy in the air.

Probably the only thing I miss about the city, Audrey said, is spring. How electrifying it is to see green after winter lets up, how everyone gets super-friendly for a minute—like for once they don't have to be über-cool New Yorkers, and they sashay around with these absolute grins on their faces.

It's the same here, Calla said. Same as it was in Vermont. Spring makes people hopeful.

Maybe that's what's gotten into me.

How do you mean?

LuLu, Audrey said. I'm smitten.

Oh, no, Calla said.

All around them lawnmowers growled, and children shrieked. A white cat with a short tail trotted out from a yard and streaked past them down the sidewalk.

I can handle it, Audrey said.

I never said you couldn't. It's just—

What?

Nothing, Calla said, pointing to a cluster of daffodils. My favorite.

Audrey shook her head. At least I let myself feel things.

Calla kept walking.

***

LuLu invited Audrey to a party at her loft.

Please come with me, Audrey begged.

Calla shook her head. She wasn't ready—the idea of people she didn't know clustering around her made her nervous.

Pretty pretty pretty please, Audrey said, clutching her hands in front of her chest.

Since when do you need an escort?

It'll be good for you to get out of the house.

I get out of the house, Calla said.

Going to work and the grocery store don't count.

I'll think about it.

Audrey hopped up and down. You're the best.

I haven't said yes.

But you will, Audrey said. I'll make dinner—what do you want?

Actually, I'm going out for dinner, Calla said. I need to get ready.

Audrey stared.

What? Calla said.

Who are you going to dinner with?

Someone I met at work.

You're going on a date. And you didn't tell me?

It's not a date. Remember the nurse when I was in the hospital, with the mismatched eyes?

Dylan? You're going on a date with Dylan?

Calm down. It isn't a date. He comes in for breakfast all the time. We've struck up—a sort of friendship.

Audrey raised an eyebrow. Okay, Miss Secretive.

Stop, Calla said.

I won't say another word.

***

She met Dylan downtown at the restaurant he'd suggested. He brought her lilacs in a Mason jar. Their heavy purple heads bobbed from the center of the table, filling the air with their scent.

Though they saw each other often, they never talked much. Calla worried, for a moment, that Audrey was right. A date. Too soon. But the snake scar hummed and purred, stirring and stretching across her belly.

It didn't take long for Dylan to start talking. Calla relaxed. She liked the cadence of his words, how he asked her questions and leaned toward her when she spoke.

She found herself telling him about her grandmother dying—almost ten years ago—how Audrey had done all the funeral arrangements, had driven them both from New York City to Wardsboro for the small-town funeral and sat next to her in the receiving line so she wouldn't be alone.

She sounds like a good friend, Dylan said.

She is, Calla said, and guilt washed over her for wanting Audrey out of the apartment, for wanting her own space back.

While they talked, she wondered if it were weird for him to sit across the table from someone whose wounds he'd tended, whose bedpan he'd emptied, whose vital stats once appeared on a chart for him to read. When he looked at her, did he remember her scar? Her blood pressure? Her painkiller dosage?

But by the end of the night she struggled against the urge to be near him, to smell him, taste him. He had a slow, graceful smile, and his eyes never left her.

The bill came, and he waved away her offer to split it. He carried the lilacs and walked her home, though he lived on the other side of town. On the porch, dim light collecting bugs in its halo, they said goodnight, and Calla let him get close enough that his stomach touched hers, and the scar did something she'd not felt before—it leapt, or seemed to, toward Dylan, had he felt it? no—his face was right there, and she turned so his mouth brushed only the edge of her lips.

She said, I can't, but he didn't move away. They looked at each other, and in his eyes was confusion. Her heart dropped, down into the scar, and it pounded there. I'm sorry, she said.

She hurried up the stairs to her apartment, relieved to find the living room dark. Tiptoeing into the bathroom, she sat on the toilet and cried. Eye makeup ran in black rivulets down her face. The scar shivered.

⚊

Calla ignored Audrey's pleas to attend the party with her until the evening Audrey came home from work, covered in cat hair and smelling like puppy piss, and said, Guess who's going to be at the party.

It's not going to change my mind, Calla said. She'd worked a double that morning, and her abdomen ached. She had slathered the scar with ointment, and still it burned.

Dylan, Audrey said, moving Calla's legs and sitting next to her on the couch. Old blue eyes.

He has one blue eye, Calla said.

One's enough, isn't it?

You can go without me. Nothing's stopping you.

When you've got nothing, you've got nothing to lose, Audrey said. She took one of Calla's feet and began rubbing it.

Quoting Bob Dylan *and* a foot massage? You're desperate, aren't you?

Please? Audrey drawled, batting her eyelashes. Pure camp. Pretty please?

Fine, Calla said. But just this once.

You're the best, Audrey said.

Yeah, yeah, Calla said. I've heard that before.

⚊

Calla followed Audrey into the loft. Music blared across the near-empty space in front of the DJ's booth. Clutches of people stood scattered around the room. It's just a party, Calla thought. I can handle it. Music coursed through her. The scar twitched. She'd swallowed a pain pill before coming—the first one she'd taken in over a month.

A woman appeared and threw her hands in the air, exclaiming and wrapping her arms around Audrey: You came!

LuLu. She wore a tube dress, her shoulders dusted with glitter so she shimmered like a disco ball. Both arms loaded with bangles, jingling and glinting.

This must be your roommate, she said, turning to Calla.

Calla extended her hand quickly, before LuLu could hug her.

LuLu dragged them to the kitchen, a corner cordoned off with curtains.

You live here? Calla asked, surveying the stack of take-out coffee cups and empty beer bottles.

Not technically, but yeah, mostly. Whatddya want—beer?

Calla held up her hands. I'm fine.

LuLu said, Really?

Really, Calla said. The racket in her stomach grew fiercer.

She can't drink because of her medication, Audrey said. I'd love a beer.

LuLu said, Oh, there's Polly and Dylan—I'll be right back. She fluttered away, hands waving with excitement.

Calla raised an eyebrow at Audrey.

What? Audrey said.

Number one: she's Ruth's doppelgänger. Number two: those bracelets are obnoxious. Number three: definitely straight.

How do you know?

I'm not blinded by lust. She's got no edge.

You're all edge, and you're straight.

Different edge, and you know it.

We'll see, Audrey said, drinking her beer.

You'll see, Calla said. *I* have already seen.

LuLu came back with Dylan and a girl with dark hair cropped close and a set of blue eyes as serious as a stun gun. LuLu said, Polly, this is Audrey—the one I was telling you about. Audrey and Calla, Polly and her brother—

Dylan, Calla and Audrey said.

Hi, he said.

This valley is so damn small, LuLu said.

Well, Lu, you do know everyone in it, Dylan said.

Don't sass me, LuLu said, swatting his arm. Let's dance.

Audrey and Polly followed her across the floor. Dylan

and Calla stared at each other. There it was again, his eyes seeing right into her. What a mess.

Are you okay? he said. You look pale.

I'm always pale, Calla said.

Fine, you look like you've seen a ghost. Do you need water?

Maybe just to sit down.

Dylan led her along the back wall, behind the DJ, to a little door, which opened into a windowless room that contained a futon and a TV.

She sat on the futon. Dylan sat next to her. His thigh touched hers, and she leaned away.

About the other night, I wanted to talk—

We don't need to, Calla said.

The music vibrated the walls. Calla wrapped her arms around her body, trying to quiet the thrashing inside her. She wanted to take off her jeans and be in her own bed with the lights out and none of this happening.

I like you, Calla.

Please, don't.

And I know you've been through a lot, but—

I can't.

Why?

It's too weird for me, too soon.

If you're worried about what I saw, you shouldn't be.

My body is ruined.

That's not true, Dylan said.

You're not a doctor. You don't know, Calla said. She pressed her hand to her scar and felt the thudding, anxious and red-tinged, inside her.

I do know.

Calla looked at Dylan, his mismatched eyes, his crooked nose, his shock of black hair. She wanted him, and she wanted him to go away. You know I'm barren? she said. That my fiancé abandoned me? That my best friend is camped out on my couch with no intention of leaving? Calla stood. The room wobbled like a funhouse mirror. She said, This is too much for me.

Dylan reached for her hand. Wait.

I can't.

She opened the door and went out into the main room.

People everywhere. Strobe lights flashing. She pushed into the crowd. Everyone was smiling, drinking, gyrating, beatific, blissful, letting the waves of sound and light wash over them, and all Calla could think of was a crash. A crash like water curling around her, sucking her under. A crash like the car skidding slow-motion across the icy pavement away from the startled deer and rolling until a tree stopped it, and the crunch and the crush and the shatter were awful and peaceful because the worst had happened, and then everything she never knew she wanted flooded out of her, dripping down while she hung suspended and waiting.

She had to get out.

Audrey was dancing with Polly in the center of the mob. As soon as she saw Calla, she stopped.

We need to go. Right now, Calla said.

Calla started for the door, Audrey behind her, but before they could get there, LuLu appeared out of nowhere—she has a knack for that, Calla thought, through the web of fear tightening around her—saying, Don't leave yet.

And Calla looked up to see Gabriel there holding LuLu's hand, and Gabriel's mouth opened and closed without a sound coming out. He'd grown a beard, looked like he hadn't slept. Calla reared back, furious, futile, the scar screaming like a banshee.

I was going to call you, Gabriel said, letting go of LuLu and grabbing Calla's arm.

Don't touch me, Calla said, yanking away. Don't you ever dare touch me again.

Calla, be reasonable.

Reasonable? Heat seared through her. She started shrieking. She was certain she would split open. The scar would rip and out would fly her feral baby, intent on mauling Gabriel's body, too.

Then Audrey clapped her hand over Calla's mouth, said, Shhh. He's not worth it.

Who are you? he asked.

Her emergency contact. Get out of our way. Audrey stepped toward Gabriel, and he flinched.

Calla, Gabriel said as she walked by. I can explain.

But Calla didn't stop. She kept her gaze forward as she followed Audrey; she didn't want to know if anyone stared.

Calla got in the passenger seat. The night was cold, and she wrapped her arms around herself. The scar lay quiet, her body a state of abandon.

That was really something, Audrey said. They were halfway home. I've never heard you scream like that.

It's done, Calla said. Over. We can go to the Goodwill. She watched the trees flash by. Above were the underbellies of new leaves, bright against the night sky.

Kitten

After Eddie came home from the hospital, I started drinking my morning coffee on the back stairs, and that's where I am, zipping my reflective vest, when I hear yowling.

The noise moves toward me across the parking lot. Black kitten—one from the brood living under the community garden shed—big yellow eyes and tail curled like a question.

Not you, I say.

The kitten crouches.

Where's your bad-luck family?

That mama and her babies—all black, all five of them. *A litter of Lucifers*, I'd said to Eddie, and to Maria, whom I'd seen throw a raspberry Danish over the fence. They'd eaten it, those cats.

But I don't see the rest of them anywhere. The kitten follows me while I walk along the blacktop and peer into the other yard, the garden plots. When I stop, it stops. When I say, What do you want? it licks its chops, scrunches its face, and meows long and thin. Fine. I'll be right back.

I set my coffee on the bottom step and take the stairs two at a time. The TV mumbles in the bedroom as I push cans around the cupboard looking for mackerel. Eddie used to make this godawful soup with it, stinking up the whole apartment. A can of beans falls and dents the linoleum, rolls away.

Carmen? Eddie calls from the bedroom.

It'll have to be tuna. Cheaper anyway.

Now Eddie's in the doorway, almost filling it. He's put on at least fifty pounds since he's been home. You okay? he asks, eyeing the can of StarKist.

There's a kitten in the parking lot.

One of the black ones? Eddie lurches forward, like he expects his missing foot to catch his weight. The crutches look like twigs under his arms.

It wouldn't leave me alone.

Get my wheelchair? He leans hard against the counter, uses one hand to smooth his hair. I want to go down.

This is the last thing I need before work, but I get the wheelchair. Eddie drops his crutches on the linoleum, hunkers into the seat, and waits for me to push him.

The elevator wheezes. The workmen were here a few days ago, cursing the trash that people throw down the shaft. Eddie's fingernails are filthy, and I don't know from what. Watching TV, eating, going to physical therapy—those are his things now. Still haven't seen him walk with the prosthesis, but he tells me he can.

Outside, his skin looks the color of a dishrag, the bags under his eyes like he's been punched. But he spots the kitten, and his shoulders straighten. Gatito, he calls, rubbing his fingertips together. C'mere, gatito.

The kitten slinks in a wide circle around us, sits down a few feet away, eyes darting.

Gimme the can, Eddie says. He pops the lid, sets the tuna next to his wheel. The kitten sniffs but doesn't budge. Aren't you hungry, little one?

The thing takes two tiny steps toward the can, stops, backs up. This could go on for hours. I walk the lot again. Behind the dumpster, along the garden fence, are three cans of cat food, empty. A cut-down soda bottle filled with water.

I call to Eddie, C'mon, I'll take you up. Joe gets mad when I'm not ready—throws the route off.

Shh, Eddie says. He and the kitten stare at each other.

You gonna be okay without me?

I'm not an invalid.

Aren't you cold? He's only got a T-shirt on, and I can see the tattoo of my name, ruined now by a scar so it only says *men*.

Where's the other ones?

How should I know?

It's weird he's alone, Eddie says, finally looking at me. Sensing his distraction, the kitten lunges forward, grabs a mouthful of tuna, takes off with it.

The bus brakes in front of the building and honks. I have to go, I say. Eddie waves me away. God, I should be used to guilt by now, but I'm not.

⁂

Eddie's parked by the fence when I get home, and Tony stands beside him, big hoop of keys hanging from his belt. They stare down a tidy row of cabbages.

Tony looks skinny as hell next to Eddie, and he leans on the fence, making kissy noises, and Eddie says something I can't hear. Tony climbs the chain-link and drops to the other side, boots shuffling amid dirt and bologna wrappers and six-pack rings and more cat food cans. He kicks the stuff away and gets down on his knees, looks under the shed.

What's going on? I ask.

Eddie flinches at my voice, but I pretend not to notice. The elevator tech took the other cats.

Tony picks up an old broom handle and says, Let's flush him.

You'll freak him out, Eddie says. We gotta get him to trust us.

I'm sure the elevator guy'll be back, I say.

I want to keep him, Eddie says.

No, I say. No way.

Why not?

You don't even like cats.

I like this cat.

Where's the love, Carmencita? Tony says, lifting his head to look at us, broom handle partway under the shed. I've told him a million times not to call me that.

Someone else is feeding it, I say.

He's been abandoned.

Mind your business, Tony. I've got my hands full.

Eddie folds his arms over his chest. Fool, quit sticking that under there. You're traumatizing him.

And pets are expensive, I say.

I'm going upstairs, Eddie says. He spins his chair and rolls toward the door.

Tony tosses the broomstick, hops the fence, and says, He'll survive.

I can't tell if he means Eddie or the kitten.

Good to see you, man, Tony calls, but Eddie doesn't turn. Then to me: We miss Eddie's face. How come he never hangs out?

Are you for real?

Shit, it's just a leg, Tony says, sauntering back to the super's office. Plentya people 'round here making do with a lot worse gone.

﹡

That night I find Eddie sitting on the bed holding the prosthesis. If he hadn't looked up and seen me, I'd've backed away and gone into the bathroom to brush my teeth. But he does look up, and I catch his unguarded hesitation before it skitters away. Reminds me of the first time I saw him naked.

Why don't you put it on? I say.

It doesn't look like a leg, Eddie says, running his thumb along the metal.

But you can walk with it, I say. Right? I haven't seen you—

It's not a real leg, Eddie says.

It's better than nothing, I say.

Don't, he says, bending forward to tuck the prosthesis back into its box. You don't get it.

I want to, I say.

What good does that do? Eddie says, grabbing the remote and turning on the TV. Will you bring me some ice cream?

Same thing he asks every night. We're lucky, I guess, that his brother works at the plant and drops by three gallons of Neapolitan every Friday.

I drift off to the sound of some rerun. There used to be real voices in the apartment: Tony, Yvonne, Johnny, Maria, Manuel. Now it's just bad jokes and tinned laughter.

Next thing I know Eddie's shouting. I touch his arm, the

way Maria told me, enough to trigger his mind away from the nightmare but not enough to wake him. He jumps out of bed with a yelp, makes it two paces before collapsing. The TV screen flickers in the dark room.

Leave it, Eddie says.

But I get out of bed and put on my wrapper. Last time this happened, Mrs. Perez knocked on the front door asking if everything was okay. The time before that, Tony showed up groggy, saying the Johnsons were worried about all the noise.

I'll heat some milk, I say.

Eddie hauls himself into bed, arranges the pillows. I go into the kitchen, pour milk in a pan, watch to make sure it doesn't scald. The microwave died a week ago, and the savings jar—the one that was going to get us a house someday —has only pennies left. I haven't told Eddie we're this broke.

By the time I carry in the mug of milk, Eddie's snoring, blankets all tangled around him. I ease the blankets back. The stump looks tender, much too weak to bear the weight it's supposed to. I haven't been allowed to touch it since Eddie first came home, doped up on pain meds. I kneel down, eye-level with the scar. Four months now since the stitches came out, and the knee still looks bruised, the skin below it puckered and pale. So light I almost can't tell I'm doing it, I run my fingertips over the scar.

Does he have both legs in his dreams? Is it like what the Sisters used to tell us about heaven: arthritis healed, eyeglasses no longer necessary, the best body returned to you? I bring my fingers to my lips, back to the scar. Eddie shifts a little but stays asleep.

After a while, I gulp the milk. It makes me queasy, but it's easier that than to watch it swirl down the drain. I suppose I could have saved it for the kitten—but no. Lucifer has to learn to make it on his own, and saucers of milk aren't going to help.

There are more empty cans of cat food by the fence, and a red plastic bowl, some string. But the kitten appears as soon as Eddie's wheels grumble over the pavement, rubbing its flanks against the dumpster, meowing until Eddie opens the can of fish, and then it eats like years have passed since its last supper.

What should we call him? Eddie says.

How about Little Lucifer?

No, for real.

For real we're not calling it anything. Don't get attached.

Pick up some mackerel on your way home?

Don't we have mackerel in the cupboard?

The kitten stops eating long enough to sniff at the gauze on Eddie's stump, blinking at the smell. Then it continues wolfing the fish.

Only one can, Eddie says.

We don't have any money, I say. I touch my pocket, the ten-dollar bill I'm supposed to stretch another four days.

But Eddie's not listening. He's bent forward whispering, Gatito, where's your mama? How you gonna make it in this nasty world all alone?

Eddie holds up a piece of paper covered in careful pencil lines. Our parking lot, the proportions perfect.

What's that for? I ask, setting down a bag of groceries.

Tony's gonna help me catch the kitten.

Eddie—

Why're you being so hard about this?

You're not listening to me, I say. We can't afford a cat.

What about my checks?

They barely cover your bills. I pull out a can and bang it on the table. Mackerel's expensive.

Eddie taps his pencil. Maybe I can find part-time work, he says.

I saw a girl behind the dumpster, I say, opening the cabinet.

Eddie sketches something onto his map.

A white girl. She had sardines.

I know, he says. I met her this morning.

She's after the cat?

She said her brother has the rest of them.

So you're going to help her? I point to the map.

Eddie shakes his head, and goes back to drawing.

The girl squats beside the chain-link, and when she hears Eddie's wheels, she stands, comes over. She says hi to me, then to Eddie, I brought mackerel—I read that kittens really love it.

Eddie lights up. Mackerel's this guy's favorite.

The girl—up close I see she's not so young, she has wrinkles at the corners of her eyes and frown lines—tilts her head. She says, I have the carrier. Do you think you can get him while he's eating?

Sure, Eddie says.

The kitten watches from behind the dumpster, meowing. God, he sounds pitiful.

The girl says, If only he wasn't so skittish. My brother said he had him, but he wriggled away.

Eddie says, his chest puffing up, He trusts me. I'll grab him; you be ready.

The girl walks down the driveway. She's got on jeans that easily cost more than my weekly paycheck, and a pair of leather boots. Even the mass of hair piled on top of her head looks expensive.

Not the type I imagine chasing stray cats, I say.

What type is that? Eddie says, turning his head sharply to look at me.

I hope it works, I say.

Eddie shrugs. We'll see.

The bus brakes at the corner. I say, Good luck.

When I pass the girl coming down the driveway with the carrier in her hand, she smiles like we're old friends.

⁂

The parking lot is empty when I get home, and the kitten sleeps in a patch of sun behind the chain-link, his fur shiny as an oil spill.

The elevator has an *Out of Order* sign taped to it. I climb the four flights wondering how Eddie got back upstairs, but the apartment is empty. No note. Maybe I should call his mother. Instead I fix a cup of coffee and sit at the kitchen table and look at the map of the parking lot. Down one side

Eddie's tiny block letters list the kitten's favorite hiding spots, the times he comes out to eat, and the words *MIRA, ACHO, CARIÑO, DARKLING, GATITO, LITTLE LUCIFER*.

The apartment is stuffy, and I open the kitchen window. Below is the dumpster, and the corner of the garden lot near the shed. Eddie must've been watching those kittens grow up all along.

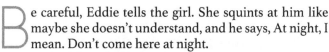

She's persistent, I'll give her that, Maria says. Grocery bags dangle from her arms as we wait for the elevator. What about Eddie? I want to say. Every morning he's down there with the girl, hatching plots: a fishing net, a milk-crate trap, putting the mackerel she brings inside the carrier and walking away. But the kitten's way smarter than both of them combined.

If by persistent you mean crazy, I say, and Maria tilts her head at me. Above, sounds like the second floor, the elevator door beeps open and keeps beeping. Are you kidding me?

Maria shakes her head, says, Girl, you're still not used to this?

I'm used to it. Doesn't mean I like it, I say. We head for the stairs. Maria lives one floor up from us—the penthouse, she calls it.

It's nice seeing Eddie around, Maria says as we climb.

It's nice having him out of the apartment, I say.

He likes that kitten, huh?

He feels bad for it—that's why he's helping her.

Maria's mouth purses, like she's thinking something she's not sure she wants to tell me. I hope they get it, she says, before she steps up the last flight.

Me, too.

Be careful, Eddie tells the girl. She squints at him like maybe she doesn't understand, and he says, At night, I mean. Don't come here at night.

I work nights, she says.

Okay, good, he says. I mean, no one'll bother you, but, just to be safe.

The girl says, One of the guys from the garden gave me cilantro the other day. I love cilantro.

I turn away, so they can't see my smile. Eddie underestimates the girl: yesterday crazy Julius got right up in her face, and she didn't even flinch. She won't leave without getting what she wants. She's spent hours behind the dumpster. Like getting this kitten is the only thing that matters in the world.

Elevator's out again. God, I'm tired of this. And waiting for eggs to go on sale and week-old baked goods and leftovers from our mothers, and barely being able to manage that. I'm banging cans onto the counter, but that's no match for whatever Eddie's doing in the other room. I don't turn when he comes into the kitchen, but I say, Why in hell are you making so much goddamn noise?

Eddie doesn't respond, but he doesn't move, either, so I look, and he's standing on two feet, holding a makeshift cage.

Oh.

He takes a deep breath and says, I'm getting the kitten. Tonight. He thumps over to the door and drops the cage.

For the girl?

Not for the girl. He crosses his arms and straightens up. She's been here every day for two weeks. If she was gonna get him, she'd have him by now.

I thought you were helping her, I say.

Maybe he belongs here.

A cat won't change anything.

Maybe we can just see, Eddie says.

I don't know, I say.

He gives the prosthesis a quick tap. It's better than nothing.

At 8:45, Tony knocks on the door, and Eddie leaves.

After getting ready for bed, I kneel on the bathroom linoleum and pray, something I haven't done since Eddie came home. My forehead pressed to the cool edge of the sink, the words run out fast: *Have mercy on us have mercy on us have mercy on us.*

What time is it? I ask.

Eddie's getting into bed. 5:30.

I have to get up.

Eddie rolls over, but I notice the bandage on his hand before he can hide it.

What happened?

Nothing.

Something, I say, pulling on his shoulder, but he won't budge.

He attacked me, Eddie says, closing his eyes. I almost had him in the cage—

Shit. You could get sick; it could have rabies.

I'm fine, he mumbles. He's nodding off quick. Tony took me to the ER.

Another bill, to add to the pile of ones still not paid. I get dressed and make coffee, study the new antibiotics on the counter.

Outside it's pouring, and the kitten peeks through the chain-link. It lets out a squeaky meow, showing its pink tongue.

No, I say. Not this time. The kitten slinks back to where the shed roof protects it from the rain.

I go down to the end of the driveway and wait for the bus there. When I get home from the morning route and coffee with my mother, the kitten's nowhere to be seen.

Eddie sits, bandaged hand resting on the kitchen table. He says, She got him.

The girl? She was here?

Eddie nods.

I go to the window and look down at the dumpster.

She sat back there for almost an hour, Eddie says.

How? Not that it matters.

Eddie hobbles over. He grimaces each time he puts pressure on the prosthesis. Some sort of sack. I didn't feed him last night—he musta been real hungry.

And cold and wet and tired.

She took off running with him. He takes a deep breath, exhales.

The warmth tickles my neck. I shiver.

You should've seen the look on her face, he says. Pure relief.

He'll have a good home now, I say.

He would've had a good home here.

We watch the rain pelt down. After a while Eddie limps toward the stove. He says, I'm gonna make mackerel soup for lunch—

I nod, and stare at the dumpster, wondering if this is what I meant when I asked for mercy.

Kintsukuroi

We're in bed when I say it—he on his stomach, eyes closed, me stretched out next to him, watching his fists clench the pillow.

If you lost your wife because of this, would it be worth it?

Something I've asked myself over and over, in those dark hours between midnight and five a.m., which is about when I exhaust enough to drift into an hour of sleep before the alarm.

Unsure, still, whose answer I fear more.

Michael strums his fingers over the curve of my hip and thigh. She won't find out. She can't.

Quiet falls over the room, only the occasional creak of the sign outside interrupting it, and Michael's hand lingers, starting the familiar swirling in my center. That feeling like when I first start forming a new piece on the wheel, how the clay yields to my hands and the centripetal force, as if already aware of its shape.

I say nothing, wait for him to return the question, but his breathing levels out, and I know he's drifted into sleep. An indulgence allowed to him only during our few hours together—he has a three-year-old and a seven-year-old at home, and a full course load, and other obligations I don't ask the details of. When he wakes, he's hungry, like a bear emerging from hibernation. Those post-nap, second-round fucks are decadent—slow and wide-eyed, inhales and exhales matching, our connection ferocious and deep, a wild blurring of bodies into a taut gold thread of ache.

She won't. She can't. His certainty doesn't surprise me. But I wonder.

I slide toward Michael, away from my thoughts. He shifts so our bodies are flush. I bury my face into his neck, nipping at his skin. He murmurs something I don't quite catch, but I think he says, You're asking for it.

***

During the winter holiday rush, Michael came through my open studio looking for coffee mugs. He picked up a salt-glazed bowl, ran his fingers along the mottled surface. He asked what type of clay I used in my stoneware, where I sourced it. Then his eyes strayed to the wall of shelves in back. What's with the broken stuff? he asked.

That— Pieces returned from friends and customers, pieces cracked in the kiln; I'd been saving them all. *Kintsukuroi*, I said.

He raised an eyebrow. He wore a thin, silver wedding band. Like mine.

Golden repair. I led him to the shelves, held out the practice bowl. Real gold, in the lacquer. You won't break it, I said, laughing. Again.

He thumbed the shimmer where cracks had been. What a noble concept, he said. Cherishing the broken. He handed the bowl back to me, and our hands touched, and neither of us pulled away quite as fast as we should have.

We talked as people floated in and out, no one brave enough to interrupt us till the woman with the long braid and brilliant-watt smile started asking a million questions about my firing process, my temperatures, my underglazes. Michael winked, took a card, and bowed out.

The woman said, He'll be back.

Lots of browsing today, I said.

She cast her gaze toward the door, then picked up a bud vase, pot-bellied with a tight-curled lip, so thin as to be almost translucent. Is this for sale?

Not really, I said. I took the vase from her hands. It felt fragile as an eggshell. My first foray into porcelain. I'm not sure how they'll fare.

The soft skin of her face was deeply lined, like she'd

walked a long way in the sun to arrive at my place. She gave me a seasoned smile. I'll take my chances.

e dress without speaking, unhurried and efficient. As I pull on my socks, Michael opens his wallet and tosses a twenty on the night table. If no one else knows, the maids in this hotel do, I think, because who else leaves such a tip for a few hours' use?

After our first afternoon together—in a much fancier place—he left a fifty. Luck had it that both Dot and Anne were out of town, and we spent hours naked between the bright-white sheets, the electric fireplace blazing, unrushed and tender, the way it is when you first discover somebody—new skin, new fingers, new taste, new breath, new rhythm—coming together and apart once, twice, three times, till we joked about my needing one of those doughnut cushions.

It'd been years since I'd been with a man, and I bled.

Am I hurting you? he asked.

No, no—

We pressed together like we wanted to dissolve our skins, and fell asleep tangled. I woke to find blood smeared everywhere: sheets, pillows, fingers, sticky along my thighs, a fierce stripe across his lower belly.

Look at this mess, I said.

Michael got a towel, and we sat crosslegged facing each other while he cleaned us. He slid the terrycloth over me, watching me as he did, till I filled all over with desire.

I said, It's like I'm a virgin again.

He laughed his rusty grumble of a laugh and called me Artemis.

Why? I said.

The virgin huntress no man can tame.

I eased the bloody towel from his fingers.

Besides, you don't seem like a Christine to me.

Only our knees touched. He traced a line from my bottom lip straight down my center into my pubic hair. I'd never felt so gutted.

I'd been glad, that dusking evening, to go home to an empty house. Michael'd gone to pick up his kids, had made them dinner and read them bedtime stories. What did it feel like, I asked, to do that? He only said, Complicated.

Now it's easier. Now the bland rooms are familiar, our habits familiar. We shrug into jackets; I rummage in my purse for keys; he hands me my hat. We hug, bodies straining against all that fabric, and though I usually go first, tonight I say, I'm not going to leave yet. If you don't mind.

He tilts his head, like he wants to ask why, but says, I have to run. Otherwise, I'll be late.

He kisses my forehead, my nose. His lips on my lips, and I want to whisper, Stay with me, but I pull away and say, Go.

Alone in the inky twilight of the room, I draw back the curtains and watch him cross the parking lot to his truck. Does he do this for me?

On the nightstand next to the twenty is a notepad and pen, and I write: *Call us selfish and dishonorable, but nothing has ever felt this pure.*

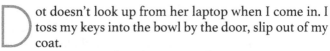

Dot doesn't look up from her laptop when I come in. I toss my keys into the bowl by the door, slip out of my coat.

How was yoga? she asks, eyes on the screen.

Backbends and arm balances, I say. A good class. How was your day?

Long. I've just got to answer these emails. Then I can help with dinner.

I can handle it, I say. Want anything special?

She says, I'm not very hungry.

Do you not want me to cook? I can graze.

She sighs and snaps her laptop shut, taps out a beat on the table, looks at me over her glasses. How about stir-fry? she says. Then, Your arms look strong.

I open the fridge door, rummage through the crisper drawers. What I want and don't want is for her to come touch my biceps, to hug me without my asking, though I count on her not doing this, not coming close enough to smell where I've been. Thank you, I say. All that throwing for the craft fair, I guess.

Nothing to do with your new yogini lifestyle?

I'm half-turned toward the counter with a tub of tofu in my hand, and we catch eyes. For the first time in what seems like ages, we smile. Maybe a little, I say. You want wine for fortification?

Not right now, she says.

She heads upstairs, and I pour a glass of red and turn on the radio and stand at the counter, staring into the dark backyard. I think about my question in the curtain-dim light of the motel, wonder if it was unfair. Dot must be on the phone; the floorboards overhead creak as she paces—the clomp of her boots against the old wood even though I ask her to take her shoes off at the door. Have always asked that, since we first met, to keep the floors clean. Her slippers lay unused in the front closet. My own feet are bare—it is late April, and still cold, but I like to feel the ground beneath me.

What would it be like, to have Michael here? Does he sit in the kitchen with Anne while she cooks? Help her chop? Play with the kids instead of zoning out on the computer? Not that it matters. He isn't mine. I put down the wine glass and close my eyes. He is not mine. But I imagine him slicing peppers, talking about minerals and aquifers, how water filters through rock, the nostalgic look he gets when he talks about digging in the earth, and there's that question again.

My answer spins like an unruly vessel, mouth too wide, walls too thin, unable to support its own weight.

I cube and sauté; I season and stir. As if I might build, with the mundane rhythms of my life, a sort of scaffolding.

Dot doesn't appear till I call for her. She rubs her eyes, says she's sorry.

For what? I ask. I pour more wine.

I'll have some now, she says, getting one of my small tumblers from the cabinet. She never uses a glass; she insists wine tastes better drunk from clay. One email after another, she says. I can't get on top of things.

I managed fine alone, I say.

As always, she says. Smells delicious.

We clink, say Cheers. I hesitate, about to add more, but Dot's already drinking, and what would I toast to right now, anyway?

see the note before Michael does and slide it into my purse while he stares out the window, then pulls the drapes. Has housekeeping left that note for the past three mornings? Has no one been in the room since we were last? Is our schedule that predictable? We've only been coming to this motel for a few weeks. Before that, we used the house of one of Michael's colleagues who was on a research trip to Istanbul. Before that, another motel. Before that, others.

My youngest has a fever, Michael tells me as he unzips his vest. I was up all night with cold cloths and Gatorade. I made up a department meeting I couldn't skip.

We could have canceled—

He slips his fingers beneath the hem of my T-shirt. And miss this?

I missed you, too, I say.

He grasps my waist, holds me a little away. Looks like he's trying to memorize me. And then he says, We should not— he reaches for my jeans zipper, tugs, eyes not leaving mine —talk this way. It makes things—

I stop his words with my mouth.

We move slow today. Michael lets me lead, on his back holding my hips, stares up at me, eyes half-closed. He whispers, You're exquisite.

Shhhh, I say.

No, I mean it, he says. You should be bronzed. I lean forward to kiss him, and it must be how I tilt my hips; he tangles his hand in my hair and draws me down so our stomachs, our chests, our mouths seal, seamless. He breathes into me, says, I'm going to—

He falls asleep almost as soon as I roll away. I trace the dark smudges below his eyes, stroke his sandpapery cheeks with the back of my hand. Naked, mouth open a little, snoring—this is what makes things difficult, I think—how much he trusts me.

I pad over to my bag and pull out the note.

I'm not God, I just clean the rooms.

What had I expected? Advice? Understanding? Absolution?

I tear the note into small squares and take it to the bathroom and toss it in the toilet, squat and pee before I flush. I do a few sun salutations, but the carpet grosses me out, so I spend the next hour thinking about my kintsukuroi project, if I'll get it done for the fair.

I get into bed and whisper, Time's up.

Without opening his eyes, Michael wraps his arms around me and holds me to him. He shivers.

You're warm, I say. Better get home and have some chicken soup.

He moans a little when he sits up. Sweat beads along his temples. If only you could bring me chicken soup, he says. In nothing but an apron.

I toss him his underwear. He doesn't budge. Here, I say, picking up his underwear from the bed, lifting his leg, then the other. Let's get you dressed and out of here.

He pulls me close again. The heat of his skin presses through my T-shirt. Not yet, he says. Those department meetings always run late.

But we don't fuck. Instead, he holds me, his chin buried in the crook of my neck, one of his legs over mine. His heart thumps against his ribs, my ribs, my heart, our flesh together soft as new clay.

The craft fair and the yoga are honest, in their way. Every week I hit the Wednesday advanced class at noon, and I'm at the wheel most spare hours—my wrists ache—which is normal enough. Dot doesn't question my whereabouts or distracted state. She has her own packed schedule: fundraisers and staff parties and volunteering and potlucks—these last I'm invited to, but decline, and she comes home with rinsed-clean bowls and hugs from the hosts, wishes for my presence next time.

She falls asleep before me. I'm up most of the night, searching for things online that only leave me empty once I see them. Dot's gone by the time I drag out of bed. I can't remember the last time she kissed me goodbye or even left a note. Maybe I'm silly; maybe I should have stopped expecting love letters years ago. Drinking coffee alone before I head to the studio, I haunt our house. The silence, the unmade bed, the pile of magazines on the coffee table. Someone lives here, we live here, but the place feels vacant. Dust on the picture frames and a pile of unopened mail and un-paid bills—my chores, neglected.

This morning, frost laceworks the windows, and sun-light wavers along the walls. Winter should have let us out of its grip by now—first week of May, and by midafternoon it'll be warm enough to shed a layer or two—but things remain frozen. I trace the crackled ice with my fingers, try to memorize the fractals. On the back of an envelope, I draw a heart and leave it where Dot will see.

By the time I get to the studio, the sun's high, and there isn't time for me to throw before I'm supposed to meet Michael. The broken pots hunker on their shelf, surly and jagged. Might as well.

In my tool cabinet sit the resin and the lacquer in their squat jars with tiny, tight Asian characters on the labels. Little bag of gold powder with a price tag that made Dot shake her head in disbelief. The process increases the object's value, I told her. An ancient practice. But she's never been one for metaphor.

And it is a process. Caught up in the filling, the smooth-ing, the dipping of the brush into the gold—I lose track of time and don't come-to till my phone buzzes. A message from Michael: *where are you?*

I'm half an hour late and don't want to leave. I text back: *studio. lost track of time. come here?*

Ten minutes later, he's locking the door behind him. We've been here together two or three times—that balding crimson velvet chair by the window finally making itself useful—but we try to avoid personal spaces, places our spouses might appear without warning.

I almost checked in, he says, but I got this strange feel-ing.

Sometimes he talks like this—though he looks like a lumberjack and doesn't believe in his wife's God, he swears by a buried intuition I can't help but be crazy for.

I'm waiting in my truck, he says, and who walks out of the lobby but one of my colleagues. Straightening his tie and looking rather satisfied, followed a few minutes later by another colleague, dazed and her shirt buttoned wrong.

We'll have to switch motels again, I say.

Michael shakes his head like he's clearing some thought

he doesn't want. I wondered, he says, if that's what we look like.

I put down the vase I'm brushing and stand. He stares out the windows, his mouth tight. He doesn't move toward me as I do toward him, and I have to turn his face. Limn his lips with my fingertips, edge him in gold. No, I say.

You weren't there, he says.

No matter what they looked like, I say. That's not us.

He turns my hands over, revealing the life line and head line and fate line, all the creases bright with gold. He says, How do we look?

Like this, I say, leading him to my worktable. I sweep the gold brush over his palms, close his fists, reopen them. I slide my palms next to his, so our heart lines align. A long road. If I blur my vision, I can close the gaps between.

How is it you're so wise? he asks.

I'm not, I want to say. It's just how I feel. That some turn at a crossroads or crossed-stars brought me to him. But words mean nothing. We stare at our palms.

Michael says, Let me help you with your pots.

I hand him clean brushes, show him the steps.

Kintsukuroi, he says, savoring the word. He learns quickly and fits the pieces together with great patience. He gives over his entire concentration to each bowl, each vase, puzzling the shards together, gliding on the gold.

No one will forgive us. No one will care how my heart swells with the sight of his clean fingernails, the dark hair curling on his forearms, the wrinkles radiating out from his eyes.

He catches me watching, says, What?

Nothing, I say. You're good.

I always wanted to work with my hands.

Why don't you, I almost ask, but there's no reason to poke a sore spot that has nothing to do with me, so instead I say, You are rather talented in that department.

First smile of the afternoon, and my ribs feel like they could shatter.

We don't go back to the motel.

Part of me regrets this; part of me is relieved. I wonder if there are unread notes in the wastebasket—notes other guests ignore, or read and interpret as they need to, like a horoscope.

We go to a different motel, but it's too shabby, too depressing. We drive up to the waterfalls and park where no one can see us. We use my studio, more often than we should.

Dot's musical goes up, and I miss all three performances because of how behind I am. She accepts my profuse apologies with cold sadness. She says, more than once, You have to get your work done, I understand.

But she doesn't. And why should she—I am plainly being unfair. She tells me after the final show that the kids got standing ovations, that it was one of their best, and I say, Next year, I'll be there. Next year, she reminds me, she's handing the reins to the assistant director.

Maybe someone videoed it, she says, drumming her fingers on the counter. I'll ask around.

The following weekend, Michael and Anne go on holiday, and I throw until my wrists turn stiff and fiery, and I have to strap on ice packs. I doze in the velvet chair and wake as the sun sets, the clear almost-summer rays spilling in the windows. I'm not usually here this late. The light illuminates the kintsukuroi pots—all lined up in a mirage of wholeness.

The weekend of the craft fair my wrists burn like they've been in the kiln, and when I drop the coffee mug that Dot hands me and scald my foot, she digs my wrist braces out of the medicine cabinet and says, I'll come with you—you're going to need help handling the money and wrapping.

I don't, but say nothing, go upstairs to my closet, and find the arm warmers she bought for my birthday last year. It's awkward to wear them over the braces, but at least the comments will be about the pretty yarn rather than questions about what I did to my wrists.

Dot hovers while I get ready, asking me what she should

wear, like she's never been to a craft fair, like it even matters. She asks if she can carry anything out to the car, and I tell her the boxes by the back door, but when I come down, she's gotten distracted by a phone call, laughing, standing by the window. I heft the boxes, slam the screen, wait in the passenger seat for her to finish, and we drive across town in silence so thick we'd need a chainsaw to cut it.

But once inside the drafty old building, I'm glad she's there. I shoulder the bags, and she unloads the car into the dumbwaiter, makes several trips to the booth, unwraps my wares, and helps me with the display.

Just before the doors open, she says, I'll grab us more coffee.

I vow to be nicer; I vow to say thank you when she returns.

She's gone for a while—probably bumped into someone from work—and my first customer is Anne. We've never met, but I recognize her the moment she appears. She's smaller in person, more delicate than I'd imagined. The room falls quiet, and blood rushes in my ears. Act normal, I tell myself.

Normal.

She picks up a kintsukuroi vase—I brought only a few, haven't even priced them—and says, This is gorgeous. How much?

I debate: tell her it's a display? name an outrageous price, five-thousand, maybe? but Dot walks toward me, holding our coffees, and the sounds of the room return, chatter, coins changing hands, kraft paper wrapping breakables, and I say, They're $75 each. Real gold in the lacquer—but they're not functional. You can't put water in it.

Anne turns the vase over, runs her fingers along the base. She says, But with a few lunaria pods—it'd glow.

I want to hate her. I want to say, I know your husband, I know that spot on his thighs that makes him quiver. But she's standing there, holding the vase out to me along with cash, and her face is so wide open and graceful; she has a crooked eyetooth and a lopsided smile.

Dot takes the vase and the money, says, Christine hurt her wrists.

Anne points at the arm warmers, says, Great cover-up.

And like I'm possessed, I extend both arms to her, palms up, and say, Cashmere.

Anne touches one wrist, then the other, says, Look at that wishbone stitch. Exquisite.

You're a knitter, I say.

Anne looks surprised, but nods. A hobby, she says. Nothing quite this lovely.

Dot hands Anne the wrapped vase, and Anne gives a little wave. She weaves through the now-crowded room. Her slim hips, the perfect straightness of her hair across her T-shirt, make me want to weep. I want to call after her: I didn't mean to love him. I never wanted this to happen.

Dot says, Here, drink your coffee. It'll help you wake up.

Michael comes to the studio Monday morning. I'm surrounded by half-unpacked boxes, my hair unwashed, my hands dusty.

What a nice surprise, I say.

He roughs his hand over his chin. Did you sell any of the pieces I did?

I didn't bring yours.

He says, It's on our mantel. First thing I see when I come in, last thing I see before leaving.

Michael, I say. It's just a vase.

Your vase. In my house.

Break it, I say. Say it was an accident.

Michael shakes his head. I can't do that.

Then what? It's not like I had a choice—

I know, he says. I'm sorry. It must have been awkward.

I remember Anne's fingers tracing the stitches of my arm warmers, her smile as she took the vase from Dot. Complicated, I say.

I never answered your question, he says.

Though it's been several weeks, I know exactly which he refers to. It wasn't fair of me to ask, I say. Loosening the straps of my braces, I tug one, then the other, off, massage my wrists, my palms.

It was fair, he says. I owe you that, at least.

We lock eyes. I hate the unknowing, the fear, I glimpse there.

I'm not in any rush, I say.

He takes my face in his hands and kisses me, gentle as the first time, lingering way too long before he lets go.

Michael parks the truck overlooking the waterfalls. He hasn't looked at me during the entire bumpy ride out here. The ticking of the engine and the water crashing down on the rocks fill me with dread. I wish we were at the motel. I wish Michael would undress me, reveal the lace bra I wear, the new underwear.

Last night was the Strawberry Moon, but Dot was too tired to sit out back with me, and I spent hours on the porch steps alone, gulping rosé with the words *where the light pours in* running through my mind. My head hurts now, the wine bottle empty and Dot grimacing as she tossed it into the recycling bin.

I could write a hundred-page list of reasons not to feel bad for myself—food deserts and abandoned children and pit bulls trained to kill, GMOs blighting our agricultural landscape and fresh water going scarce, drone attacks and homeless veterans and stray cats—but here I am in the passenger seat of this F-150, wishing I had aspirin and a soft pillow, wishing Michael would pry my fingers apart and kiss me instead of clenching the steering wheel.

He says, I've been thinking—

I stare at the riot of green leaves, sunlight filtering down in watery bars.

He says, We have to stop.

You could leave Anne, I say. I'd leave Dot, for you.

Christine, he says. We can't be responsible for that kind of wreckage.

A woodpecker takes up hammering somewhere nearby. In my peripheral vision, I see Michael reach for my hand, but he draws back when I make no motion.

I hear him say, I'm sorry.

Please, I say.

I can't, he says.

I know, I say.

I'm sorry, he says again.

Please, stop saying that.

We've been reckless, he says. Selfish.

I crack the window, afraid the heat inside my chest will ignite, sending splinters in every direction.

Michael grips the steering wheel. Damn it, he says. Nothing feels right.

Stop, I want to say. Stop.

When I first saw you, in your studio, I thought some piece of me might crumble if I never held you or tasted you or breathed you. I shouldn't have—I couldn't resist you.

Don't.

I can't leave Anne, he says. I made a promise to her; I want to be there for my family. I couldn't live with myself— knowing I'd hurt them.

Why, then? I want to ask. Why?

Christine, he says, turning in his seat, cupping my cheek so I have to face him. Forgive me. I wish I trusted my heart the way you do.

I lift my hand to cover his, pressing my cheek into his palm. For a long time, we stay like this. Until I release him and say, Take me back.

In the studio parking lot, Michael cuts the ignition, and we stare into the thicket of brambles that edge the pavement. We do not kiss; we do not say goodbye. I hope he'll do something, anything, to change this moment. He takes my hand in his and turns it, traces the lines of my palm.

We'll find a way to live with this, he says.

I meet his eyes—they mirror my own, exhausted and shell-shocked and dry. I'm not so sure about that, I say.

We will, he says. We'll scar up.

But how deep the line he cut down the center of me, how long it will take to heal. I think of the gold smeared on our life lines, our fate lines, our heart lines.

We're strong, he says. We have to be. He closes my fingers and holds my fist between his two hands.

With my free hand, I press a finger to my lips, then to his. Don't leave me, I want to say.

But already I can see how we shine.

climb into my car, arrive home with no recollection of the drive, compose my face in the rearview.

Dot's on the couch, bare feet on the coffee table, watching a music video on her computer. She glances up at me, says, You're early. What happened?

Nothing, I say. Not feeling well.

Too much wine last night, she says with a ghost of a smile.

Not that, I say. A cold, maybe. Summer flu.

You're pale, Dot says. Go get in bed. I'll bring you chicken soup.

No soup, I say, closing my eyes against the sunlight flooding the room. All I want is to go upstairs and pull the shades and slip between the cool sheets of darkness. I need to rest.

Okay, Dot says, turning her attention back to the screen. You should have come home sooner.

Seal

All I want is to eat my lasagne and drink cabernet and listen to talk radio, but Stella's got her eye on me as I twist the corkscrew, and when I reach for the wine glass, she says, I thought you were quitting.

December first, and a thin skin of ice drapes Brooklyn. Stella has drawn the curtains against the darkness. The radiator clanks, hissing steam into the kitchen. A customer dined-and-ditched, and I had to pick up the tab out of my tips, and I turned 30 last week, and I'm failing the philosophy class I'm taking in the city because half the time I'm too tired to get on the subway. I should be there right now, and I'm sure the professor is duly noting my absence with another black mark.

But here I am, defending the uncorked bottle: A glass isn't going to hurt—we don't even know if it took. Which, as far as I know, it did not, because this morning I peed on a stick, and only one line darkened. I'm not bleeding, though, or even crampy.

You promised you'd be sober through this.

Can I have one last indulgence, please? Which isn't the best argument, given my mother overdosed on pain meds eight years ago today, after being diagnosed with cirrhosis and refusing to give up her nightly triple martini.

I'm not an alcoholic, but when Stella and I first met, a year after my mother died, I convinced her to rent a car and drive to Northampton, my hometown, three hours north of Brooklyn. While in town, we ran into a high school friend of mine at a bar—Rocco, who used to go by Rachel—and I proceeded to get so drunk that I blacked out in the bathroom, fell, and chipped my front tooth and split my bottom lip. Stella and Rocco carted me to the emergency room where I got two stitches and a warning from the doctor about alcohol poisoning. Stella stayed stoic, but when we got back to the city, she said, *I like you, but I can't deal with this.* And I knew what she meant, and for once I was smart enough to say I was sorry and that it wouldn't happen again, and it hasn't.

We made a deal, the first night we spent scrolling through possible sperm donors: I'd go dry to have the baby, and we'd leave the city to raise our family.

There's a difference between indulgence and coping mechanism, Stella says.

Do you want some? I ask, and Stella shakes her head, possibly in disbelief, possibly saying no. I add, The more you drink, the less there'll be for me.

Fine, she says, but remember your promise.

You don't have to keep reminding me. I'll keep to my end of the bargain.

Speaking of, can we not bring that up around Agnes?

Why not?

You know how she is.

I do, and I'd be lying to say I hadn't been wondering how I might use that to my advantage.

I just want to enjoy the holidays without all the opinions, Stella says.

Holidays in Stella's lexicon mean winter solstice and Yule parties, where everyone dresses in white and eats rosemary-caraway biscuits and burns candles to welcome back the light. This will be my fifth celebration with the hippies, and we've never once escaped without someone echoing Agnes' entreaties to move west.

Maybe Agnes is right, I say.

Oh, goddess. Not you, too.

Built-in babysitter, I tease. Sort of.

Enough, Stella says. Let's enjoy dinner.

Avoidance is Stella's thing. I like to blame her meditation practice as the means by which she blocks out reality, but I'm pretty sure it's deeper. I'm tempted to say, You promised, but I also want to drink, so I raise my glass and say, To the maybe-baby, and as I sip I think about how soon we'll be out of the freezing hustle, and my stomach warms in anticipation.

The next morning, I pee on another stick, and there they are: two blue lines. I pee on one more, because what're the chances? Two again. I call Stella at work and leave a message, and an hour later I hear her unlocking the front door.

What are you doing home? I ask when she rushes into the kitchen.

She says, Are you serious? We have to celebrate.

I say, We have to go to the doctor and get a blood test. It could be a false positive.

But we go out for ice cream anyway. It's snowing a little, and the streets look pretty, and I like walking up Ninth holding Stella's hand, cone in the other. When we get home, Stella empties the half-bottle of cabernet down the sink and rounds up the bottles of gin and bourbon, puts them in a cloth bag. When I ask what she's doing, she says she's giving the contents of the liquor cabinet to Brad at work.

That seems unnecessary, I say.

She says, He's giving his two weeks on Friday to go free-lance—he'll need it more than we do.

The blood test is positive, and morning sickness soon has me hugging the toilet bowl as often as I did in college. At work, the smell of garlic makes me dry-heave, and I have to lie down on bags of flour when work is slow. Holidays by the Bay, with no persnickety diners to fake-smile for, have never looked so enticing.

The night before we leave, I go into the pantry and dig out my mother's silver flask, engraved with her initials. Maybe it's a silly superstition. When I come into the bedroom with it, Stella says, Kristen— but I turn it upside down.

Empty.

Stella says, What do you think will happen if you leave

it here?

Humor me, I say, and tuck it in between my sweaters. I'm still keeping my word.

Stella snaps out a shirt, folds, then rolls it tight, and adds it to her pack. Getting any information out of her in regard to her end of our deal has proven impossible the last couple weeks, and I'm too worn out, knowing our flight takes off at 5:30 a.m., to push it any further tonight.

JFK to SFO has me white-knuckling a barf bag, wishing I could order the wine that usually settles my nerves. I must look pretty haggard when we disembark because the lady Stella buys an orange juice from gives me a look of deep sympathy and says, Flying is for the birds.

I choke down a sip of juice that burns through my esophagus. Walking toward baggage claim feels like a never-ending journey.

Agnes' ritual is to meet us, even though she doesn't own a car, and we'll take the bus to Sausalito together. And there she stands, by carousel number four, tall as Stella and slim-hipped, same wide gray eyes, though Agnes' hair is bright white instead of straw-colored, and her smile isn't lopsided like Stella's. She wears a long blue and purple dress and gathers Stella into her arms, kissing her messy hair. Then Agnes hugs me, lifting me off the ground.

Stella says, Be careful, in the sharp way she only has with her mother.

Agnes sets me down and smiles. Kristen, you are radiant.

Which is not even remotely true, so I know she knows, and Stella knows she knows, but none of us says a word. The little bubble, the maybe-baby turned growing cluster of cells, feels as delicate as a raw egg inside me, like any rash move might crack it.

When the houseboats come into sight—they bob along the edge of the bay and out into the water like bath toys—I'm near ready for Rip Van

Winkle-style sleep. Stella's lugging my suitcase and her pack, and Agnes has my carry-on, and still my body must weigh a thousand pounds. They're walking slowly for me, discussing Agnes' recent renovation, part of which turned Stella's room into a guest room.

It's what you mainly are at this point, honeybee, Agnes says.

Stella says, I know, but what if— and then stops herself. What if what?

Nothing. You're right, there's no need to keep my things around gathering dust.

Agnes' boat is painted aquamarine, and the railing abutting the dock is crowded with terra cotta pots filled with succulents. More color than I've seen all month in New York, where the dullness lingers like a bad hangover.

To walk up the little plank to the boat, to step into its crowded, plush interior, to sit at the metal table in the windowed kitchen overlooking the water, is like visiting another planet. It smells of chamomile tea and incense, briny oceanwater and a bit of diesel, but today I also catch an undercurrent of fish. It makes me want to gag.

This has been Stella's life since she was a kid, and as I watch her take in the cleared-out version of her teenage bedroom, nodding approval, I wonder if this is why she's resisting our move. This piece of her she thought she'd said goodbye to, and here I am, asking her to return. Full circle, and maybe she's not ready to close the gap.

L ast year I took a train to Buffalo to meet my dad, Louis, for the first time. We sat in an old-fashioned diner, the clink of silverware and shouts of *Order up* around us. I chose somewhere impersonal because I did not want to be introduced to his wife, Jacqueline. I didn't want to see where he lived. He pulled from his wallet a picture of me as a baby. Behind the photo of me was a photo of a beautiful teenage girl, dark hair parted down the middle, wearing a printed cotton skirt like the ones the hippie kids in Northampton favored.

Who's that? I asked.

Amber. My other daughter. She's twenty-eight. Lives in the city like you.

What do you say when the father you haven't seen since you were a toddler tells you he has another daughter, only one year younger than you are? It was awkward enough to notice his dark eyes and heavy lashes, his slender spoon-shaped fingers; mine, exact replicas. Louis hired a private detective to find me because once my mother died and I left Northampton, there was no one keeping track of me. I spent much of my adult life thinking I were an orphan, and then suddenly Louis' voice was on my voicemail asking me to call him back. I wanted to yell, Where were you? But Stella said I might regret it if I didn't return the call.

Why didn't you stay in touch? I asked him.

I tried. Your mother—

What?

She sent all my letters back, once every year, unopened.

My mother refused to talk about Louis, forbade me from asking about him, destroyed all his evidence.

What about pursuing custody? I didn't know why I was pushing. What's done is done, the past unchangeable. What did this man's choices matter, now that I was old enough to take care of myself?

Louis' scraggly eyebrows knit together. He looked concerned. I'm sorry, Kristen. Veronica was formidable, as I'm sure you know. And I hadn't exactly been an angel.

She went bankrupt. Booze, cigarettes, designer dresses, I said. I didn't tell him the rest, that she left me with nothing but an apartment full of moth-eaten silk and antiques so ill-treated that the auction house could barely be persuaded to take them away. She called me Krissy and slept through my high school graduation, and some days I still wish I could call her up and say, I love you.

It must have been hard on you, Louis said, placing his hand over mine on the worn Formica. To watch her destroy herself.

How rude would it be, I wondered, to move my hand? I wasn't even home when she did it, but I couldn't tell him that. It was, I finally managed.

He is my DNA, my blood. It means something, I'm sure.

Even though I'm tired, I tell Stella and Agnes I need fresh air and head out to walk along the bay. Everything is different here, the air and the light and the greenery. The water sparkles, unlike the dull chop of the rivers in New York.

Louis'd extended a welcome to us for Christmas this year, but I said no, without even mentioning it to Stella. She would have declined, too, I tell myself. He was just being nice; he knows I have other plans.

The truth is, I didn't want to go to Buffalo, still don't want to meet my half-sister or stepmother, because I don't like the idea of them being family. Stella would call this stubborn, or spiteful, and I can't explain it to her otherwise. I'm not sure I can reconcile the fact of biology with all those years of absence. I am my mother's daughter, after all.

It's my mother I'm thinking of when I see a head pop up in the bay. A harbor seal. Its large, dark eyes as liquid as the water it swims in. It ducks under, then resurfaces, ducks under again, splashing water with its tail. Droplets fly up, glittering. I get as close to the edge as I dare. The seal comes closer and regards me for a long moment—like it wants to tell me something. It ducks under once more, and I wait for it to resurface. When it does, it is heading away.

My mother pretended Louis didn't exist until I started asking if I had a dad. And even then, she remained vague. I was too young to understand the stories I overheard Veronica telling her friends: screaming matches, throwing things, broken bottles and broken dishware, and one morning, the big Tiffany lamp in a shattered rainbow across the floor. By the time I was old enough to really get it, Veronica's friends had disappeared, too.

For the last year, I've fought an unfair anger over how the cards were dealt: that Louis got clean and found peace, while Veronica got a pickled liver and shaky hands. But I know, as I watch the seal swim out to the depths, that Veronica had choices, and she made poor ones.

I walk till I hit the strip of restaurants and boutiques that comprises Sausalito's downtown. Probably too far, given my energy level, but I don't want to go back to the houseboat yet, either. The sun's an orange egg sizzling into the water, and the light refracts off the zinc oxide sign of a little bar Stella and I have stopped in on other visits. A glass of wine won't hurt, I reason, and Stella's not here to argue; I step in to warm up for the walk back.

One sip and I choke. The bartender looks confused, asks if the cab has cooked. I shake my head, pushing the glass away. He goes to pour me another, but I say, No, not that. I'm a little jetlagged, I guess. He frowns, asks if I'm sure. Yes, yes, I say, tossing him a twenty before I scramble for the door. Out into the damp evening, I suck in fresh air, my stomach wobbling from the near miss.

On Agnes' houseboat, secrets don't exist. She is a licensed psychic, after all. None of the doors, not even the front one, has a lock. Why we're trying to hide the cell takeover happening in my gut is a mystery to me.

But then again, so is Stella's and Agnes' relationship. What I know of mothers is passive aggression and slurry emotions and helplessness. But here, there are the long arguments, which they call discussions, about war and religion and the overall dismal state of the country. And at least once, every visit, they bicker over Stella's Buddhism. You wouldn't think that'd be a point of contention, but it is. Agnes calls it as organized and patriarchal as any other religion, and Stella tells her she has no idea what she's talking about, and Agnes says, I didn't raise you that way, to depend on doctrine, and Stella groans and says, Yeah, you raised me to chant in circles around fires, and then Agnes says something like, The only way you could betray me further is if you went Catholic. This, over the years, has developed into my cue to say, Don't worry, they wouldn't have her, after which everyone has a good laugh. There's a lot of laughter, actually, and a lot of expectation—neither of which feels familiar to me. Yet. Though I'm trying.

As expected, when I push through the front door, Agnes and Stella sit in the kitchen debating. Stella pounds the table and says, Mother, please, and I know it must be serious because Stella calls Agnes by her proper name unless she's annoyed.

But Agnes is near luminous with excitement. She says, Stella tells me you want to get the hell out of New York. Then, pushing out a chair and gesturing for me to join, It's about time.

We're discussing it, I say.

But?

Stella says, Don't start with the buts. We just got here. Stella leans over to kiss me, and I turn my face away. She pauses, a slight stutter. Maybe you should go lie down, she says. You're tired.

Of the noise, the trash, the empty checkbook, the crowded rush-hour trains, sure. I say, But Stella's resisting my urge for someplace new.

New like the Bay? Agnes asks.

Stop putting ideas in her head, Stella says.

Too late, I think, but I say, You know, maybe I will rest for a little while, and head to Stella's old bedroom to let them duke it out.

Agnes, like Stella, eats simple meals composed primarily of vegetables. My stomach is hollow, and the only thing I'd really care for are crinkle fries from Coney Island, but I chop radishes as directed for the salad, tossing them into a bowl hewn from a piece of redwood by Tom, Stella's father, back when they lived on a commune up north. Agnes loves to rehash Tom.

Goddess, he was beautiful back then, she says, a thing I've heard her say innumerable times, always with nostalgia. I've not met Tom, but Stella tells me he's the sort of man whose desires and pursuits change daily. He's been a father, a Buddhist, a sculptor, a screenwriter, a real-estate agent, successful at none of them. Stella and her twin brother, Wolf, have Agnes' last name on their birth certificates.

He's still beautiful, Stella says, setting down a bowl of rice.

All those spa treatments, eh?

Now now, Agnes, Stella says.

Tom has found a wealthy woman and lives as a happily kept man, and Agnes can't get enough of tearing this situation down. Last year, Stella went to visit Palm Springs and came back to New York complaining. *They eat meat for every meal and have servants and wear cashmere underwear. It's ridiculous.* Of course, Stella lives like Thoreau at Walden and loves it. She's built for minimalism, physically and mentally. She's lean and spare, one shade softer than severe—takes the subway everywhere and won't even consider taxis, grows herbs in old yogurt containers on our fire escape, gets her boots resoled at the cobbler in Red Hook.

You'd think she'd be dying to get out of New York where everything is obsessed with new and bigger and faster and more. And yet.

Around the table, Agnes grabs my hand and Stella's, and Stella takes my other hand so we form a circle, and Agnes blesses the food. *Mother Earth, who brings to us this food; Father Sun, who makes it ripe and good; dear earth, dear sun, by you we live, our loving thanks to you we give. Blessings on this meal.* This is as close to grace as I ever get.

I choke down a few bites of tofu, have better luck with the salad, pass up the broccoli that Agnes insists is good for my bones. She's on to us, and I know it, and I know Stella knows it, but I keep quiet just the same. This is, after all, Stella's and my argument to have, and it doesn't seem fair, to either of us, to allow anyone else in on it.

Wolf is sitting on the old floral couch with Stella and Agnes when I wake up and drag myself to the living room. They can't stop staring at one another, all exhilarated that they are in the same state, in the same city, in the same house, even though it happens every year for winter solstice. I like Wolf. He is handsome and unassuming, with the open face and gray eyes that run in the family.

I perch on Stella's armchair, wondering if she'll tell them now about the baby, but the topics run toward Rumsfeld's resignation and glaciers melting and how ridiculous rent has become in San Francisco proper.

Agnes finally stands. How about a hike under the Golden Gate? she asks with so much enthusiasm I could barf. Or maybe that's morning sickness again.

Wolf says, You've got more energy than a kid.

Getting lazy in your old age? Agnes ribs.

Hardly, Wolf says.

Because you can stay home.

Can I? I ask, and they all turn to gape at me. I had a long work week; I could use some down time. Especially before the ceremony.

Normally, Stella would push me, but instead she rubs my arm and says, Of course. You need your rest.

Agnes says, Kristen, why don't you help me make breakfast. These two— she waves dismissively at Stella and Wolf, can go get dressed. In the kitchen, Agnes says, My girl's got a hard head. Doesn't want to be like her father, which manifests in resisting change.

She keeps promising, but I don't know, I say. A little knot twists in my stomach. I want this baby as much as Stella does, but what if she doesn't keep her word? Not that staying in the city would be the worst thing, I say. But, you know—

I do, Agnes says. But don't coddle her. Sometimes she needs a push.

That's not really my style, I say.

Agnes hands me a block of tempeh to crumble. You're not the one resistant to change.

I nod and busy myself with the tempeh, breaking it apart and cringing at the nutty scent when Agnes grabs a handful to form a patty.

It gets better, she says. You'll see.

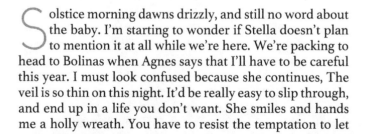

Solstice morning dawns drizzly, and still no word about the baby. I'm starting to wonder if Stella doesn't plan to mention it at all while we're here. We're packing to head to Bolinas when Agnes says that I'll have to be careful this year. I must look confused because she continues, The veil is so thin on this night. It'd be really easy to slip through, and end up in a life you don't want. She smiles and hands me a holly wreath. You have to resist the temptation to let things happen to you.

I carry the wreath out to the borrowed Toyota, wondering if I'd have more of a backbone if Agnes had been my mother. I head inside to grab my own bag—double-checked to make sure the flask was still inside—thinking that if Agnes were my mother, I wouldn't have to tote such a silly talisman around. Not that it matters. We all have our attachments. Even Stella, who thinks she's transcended the power of objects, can't go anywhere without her zafu. Comfort, my ass. She calls it practice, but I know an avoidance technique when I see one.

Once the rusty wagon is loaded, we drive up the 1, singing along to old Joni Mitchell cassette tapes. Wolf drives because Stella doesn't want to, and Agnes, like me, doesn't have a license, though I would guess hers didn't get revoked because of crashing a friend's car into a tree at the age of 19 after a night of heavy drinking. I haven't driven since and have no plans to. Stella doesn't know about the accident or how I was told I was lucky to survive. She thinks I let my license lapse after moving to the city, and I've never felt any need to enlighten her otherwise. If we move west, I wonder, will I have to come clean?

As we unload beneath the redwoods, I feel, like I always do here: tiny. An ant. Like I'm the most insignificant creature ever to step on this earth.

Ocean waves crash below, the tide rolling in, the noise rising to the yurt where we'll be camping out for the night. Agnes' friend, Jade, is a longhaired widow with watery green eyes and a wavering smile. She looks as if the damp air has entered every pore and plumped her from the inside out, no wrinkles on her placid face. We're the first to arrive for the celebration, and she takes Agnes' arm and leads her up to the main house. Something about yarrow poultice.

Stella and Wolf carry everything into the yurt, and then Stella comes out with her face vacant of any emotion, which is, truthfully, how she's spent most of this trip in regard to me, and says, Let's go for a walk.

Sure, I say and remember the seal from the other day. I never told her about it, but given that she won't meet my eye as we head down to the shore, I can't see that I want to now. I keep a lookout on the water, though, hoping for more.

About the wine, Stella finally says.

I didn't drink it, I say.

She rubs her forehead. Was I imagining the smell?

I— but what can I tell her that doesn't sound ridiculous? I took one sip. I choked. I'm sorry.

Stella looks out over the waves, wind whipping hair across her cheeks. You're pregnant, and you promised.

So did you.

Stella blends with the landscape, her shirt the same silver-green as the beach grass. Even her body, the angular length of it, fits here. I did, she says. I'm worried it's too much.

Her words deflate me. What's too much—the baby?

I'm worried about moving while you're pregnant. All that stress.

I'm already stressed.

What about work? Our friends? What about your dad?

I thought we agreed the city is no place to raise a kid.

I guess I thought you might change your mind, you know, once it took.

I touch my belly, which feels as choppy as the surf. I say, I want this.

Stella stares at the horizon, her expression unreadable. Agnes will be so happy, she says.

I want to say, And what about you? But before I can gather the nerve, she walks away up the beach and climbs the wooden stairs. I keep along the water, despite the chill, hoping for another seal. As if I might find an answer in its liquid black eyes.

At dusk, we light the candles. Agnes starts the chant, and the others join in. She leads us in honoring the darkness and welcoming the light. She asks us to witness the shadow side, to understand its usefulness, to remember that without it, the light has no meaning. The candles flicker to the cadence of Agnes' voice, and there's this little twitch in my gut. I know the baby isn't more than a poppy seed, that there's nothing, at this point, for me to feel beyond my own hunger, but the flutter doesn't let up. I press my hand over it, wondering what it wants—wondering what, after all, I want.

When we're done in the circle, we break to eat and revel around the fire. I can't stop thinking about the flask, and finally I retrieve it from the yurt. Stella's watching me as I come back toward the fire, and she squints to see what I'm carrying. Has she always been watching so intently? Have I been dancing with shadows all this time, obscuring my own vision? I hold the flask out to her.

What's going on? Stella asks, taking it.

I'm giving this to you, for now.

Kristen, you don't need to—

I made a promise.

Stella rubs the engravings with her thumb and exhales the same way I hear her do after a long meditation session, then says, Farewell, New York City.

We can visit. Maybe head to Buffalo for the holidays. Then, either with relief or fatigue or hormones, I start to cry.

You're really sure of this, aren't you?

I nod, too overwhelmed to say more.

Stella wraps her arms around me and says, I shouldn't have doubted.

The next morning, groggy and smelling of woodsmoke, we reload the Toyota and drive north to the state park. The trees are massive, deep red like brick and as solid. I stand and look up, look up the way I used to into my mother's unknowable face, but here I find awe, not fear.

Agnes says, Let's hug the tree.

She's been jubilant and overprotective since we broke the news. I almost laugh, thinking she's joking, but Stella and Wolf take my hands, and we form a circle around the base of the tree. I press my cheek, my belly, against the rough bark and exhale. Nothing has ever felt so real.

We stand this way until Agnes, then Stella, then Wolf, start chanting. I don't know the words, and for once I don't let it bother me. The deal is sealed. I let the vibration fill me, buoying the bubble in my belly. I'll learn.

Free

They walked the dirt shoulder of Route 100 leaving Wardsboro, packs strapped tight and thumbs out. Dawn a hint of pink stretching the horizon, and Calla wiped the sweat from her upper lip. She said, If you keep that up, no one's gonna stop, but Audrey kept belting, *Freedom's just another word for nothin' left to lose*—

Calla touched her back pocket, the stiff fold of directions there. For the last three nights, she'd fallen asleep incanting the routes. She watched Audrey's broad shoulders. Up ahead loomed the town line, and Calla steeled to say, Let's go home. Skip this crazy plan and spend the weekend with your parents at the lake house. No camping gear, no hitching to practically Canada, no lying to my grandmother. She could see Audrey's hands on her hips and her scrunched disappointed face, could almost taste the relief of heading back the way they came, when the Buick slowed and pulled off.

Calla quickened her pace to stay close behind Audrey, who hurried toward the rolled-down passenger window. Over Audrey's shoulder, Calla saw a dreadlocked girl with a round, flat face nursing a baby.

The driver leaned over the gearshift. Where you off to this fine morn? he asked. He had dreadlocks, too, little wire-rims, a few grays at his temples.

If you could get us to Route 9, however far east, Calla said.

Sure thing, hop in. When they made no move, he added, I'm Jim, and this here's Reina. The girl offered a sleepy smile.

Audrey flashed their all-clear, index and middle finger low against her thigh. The car shone, dark as a hearse, without a speck of mud or dust. Not exactly a reason to reject a ride, or not one to vocalize on the side of the road while two strangers waited, and the baby took up fussing.

Reina murmured, Shhshhhshhh ... Fellow travelers ... Lending a hand ...

Calla flashed her eyes at Audrey, mouthed, You sure? and Audrey slid off her pack.

The car reeked of patchouli and pot, pine air freshener, sour milk. Calla wedged in between Audrey and the car seat, legs crammed around her pack; she searched for a seatbelt, found none, figured it didn't matter. She couldn't move if she tried.

Reina thought you two looked safe enough, Jim said, pulling back onto the road.

Reina turned and smiled again. Not sleepy: dazed or melancholic-mellow. Calla knew the look well, had seen it on plenty of her friends. And Reina, Calla realized, was probably their age—her skin almost as smooth as the baby's, who was now at her shoulder, searchlight-saucer eyes settling on Calla.

Boy or girl? Calla asked.

Reina said, Baby girl.

Nameless, as yet, Jim added.

Nothing feels quite right, Reina said.

Six months of calling her Little One. Jim caught Calla's eye in the rearview, gave a slight shake of his head.

Calla looked to the baby, her dark lashes clumped with wetness. Her stare unnerved Calla; she seemed frightened, anxious. Maybe she just needed to burp. Calla didn't know.

Audrey said, We really appreciate the ride.

Where you off to? Jim asked. Final destination, I mean.

Limestone, Maine, Audrey said. We're on our way to The Great Went.

You're in luck, Jim said with a grin in the rearview. We're headed there, too.

No way, Audrey said, poking Calla's thigh.

A string of spit-up bubbled down the baby's chin. Reina wiped her with a grubby bandana. Calla wriggled as best she could away from Audrey, pulled the sheet of directions from her pocket. Luck wasn't a word she liked much.

I wrote out the way, Calla said, offering the directions. The baby grabbed them.

I know the way, sister, Jim said, popping a cassette into the tape deck. You sit back. Enjoy the journey.

Calla unlatched the baby's fingers, refolded the paper. There was still the journey home.

T he Welcome to New Hampshire sign blurred past, the car smoky now, and Calla's head fuzzed. She reeled in the words *This is the first time I've left Vermont* before they escaped. She didn't want to sound simple, and besides they weren't true. She'd been born in Montana, not that she remembered any of it, having been toted home as a toddler by her grandmother, her mom dead in a car wreck, her father long gone.

New Hampshire didn't last long, green and unremarkable, and when Welcome to Maine reared into view, Jim tapped the steering wheel, said, Gotta stop for fuel—y'all ready for a stretch?

Finally, Calla thought, her bladder cramped and burning.

The gas station looked straight out of Wardsboro, two pumps and a man in grease-smeared coveralls keeping an eye from the stone office. Several rusty Subarus and Vanagons waited to fill up.

Calla handed Jim a twenty, said, Is this enough?

Jim took the bill, considered it, gave it back. Ride's free.

We insist, Calla said, looking around for Audrey. There she was, coming out of the building with a push-up pop.

It's not like we're going out of our way, Jim said.

Audrey rummaged in her pocket, brought out a handful of ones. Here, for the gas fund.

Jim waved them off. Consider this me paying a karmic debt, he said.

Calla still had the twenty between her fingers, her arm extended, but Audrey crumpled the ones back into her pocket. Calla said, I don't like to owe anyone.

Jim eyed her, said, I get that. How about you help us take

care of the little one when we get there?

Calla scrambled for a polite decline, but Audrey said, Deal, and high-fived Jim.

The car at the pump drove away, and Jim hopped in the driver's seat to pull forward.

Calla grabbed Audrey's arm, hissed, You're insane.

Audrey eased out of Calla's grip.

Wait, Calla said. Come to the bathroom with me. Inside, Calla bolted the lock, said, This is a terrible idea.

What, the baby? Audrey said. Relax. How hard can it be for a free ride?

Calla squatted over the dirty seat. It's not— She rattled the toilet paper dispenser, empty. Hand me a paper towel.

Audrey reached, said, You're gonna have to drip dry.

Calla groaned. She wanted to strangle Audrey. Last month they'd been chased off private property with a shotgun, naked. Audrey owed her a pair of jeans for that one. There'd been the broken arm, the poison ivy, the embarrassed march into the general store to return stolen tubes of lip gloss and bag balm.

Audrey reached into her pocket, tossed her a crumpled napkin, smeared with orange from her pop. Better than nothing. We've babysat before, she said. It's an adventure.

How many times had she heard that? Calla thought as she fastened her corduroys. But maybe Audrey was right. How tough could a weekend with a six-month-old be? She is pretty cute, Calla said.

Who, Reina? Audrey teased.

Maybe they'll let us name her, Calla said.

Must you name everything you come across?

Calla shrugged, cranked the faucet. A trickle of rusty water.

You ready? Audrey asked, reaching for the lock.

Calla wiped her hands on her corduroys, said, As I'll ever be.

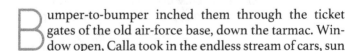

Bumper-to-bumper inched them through the ticket gates of the old air-force base, down the tarmac. Window open, Calla took in the endless stream of cars, sun glaring off windshields, flags tied to antennae, damp late afternoon wind, jangling guitars and mish-mashed lyrics from all the radios, shouts, laughter, doors slamming. The air smelled of gasoline and hot pavement and unwashed bodies. Tents sprouted like mushrooms up the center strip of trampled brown grass. On the horizon, beneath clustering rain clouds, a line of abandoned buildings that looked like bunkers.

Calla climbed out of the car, lifted her arms to stretch; her vision went blotchy, and her neck tingled. Pre-faint. She'd not eaten enough. The noise and the heat crushing around her. She got back in the car, shut the door. She gripped her knees, took several deep breaths. Don't freak out, she whispered. The baby cooed, startling her from her panic. Calla rolled down the window, said, Um, the baby?

But Jim unloaded the trunk, and Reina had sauntered a few cars down, calling, Ganga gooballs.

Audrey looked back from where she leaned on the front bumper. Get out here, and taste the madness, she said.

I've already tasted it, Calla thought, turning to the baby. She wiggled the car-seat buckle, leaning forward to inspect the jammed button, and the baby grabbed a fistful of her hair. Oowwee, Calla yipped, and the baby yanked harder. Let go, Calla pleaded, unwrapping the baby's sticky fingers, not fast enough—the baby kept reaching, getting tangled. Calla gave up, went back to the car-seat, which finally gave way. She backed out of the car with the baby gripped firmly, a handful of hair stuffed into the child's mouth.

Someone likes you, Jim said. He unhooked the baby's fingers, offered Calla a hair elastic. You'll need this. And this. He slipped a canvas sling over her head, tightened the strap. You okay with her for now?

The baby burrowed her cheek against Calla's chest. Maybe it was her weight, or her warmth, that loosened Calla. Maybe she needed a shield. We're good, Calla said, hoisting her pack. Have baby, will travel.

Jim nodded, a full body bob, said, That's the spirit.

Calla followed Audrey who followed Reina who followed Jim, trekking through the tents on the lookout for a spot. How about here? Jim asked three times before Reina nodded in agreement. Calla and Audrey said nothing: one patch of scrubby grass looked the same as the next.

The spot Reina chose was beside two tents pitched by laidback college guys who shared their beer, cold bottles fresh from the cooler, pearled with condensation. Calla sipped the one handed to her—she didn't love the bitterness, but thirst won. She had no idea where to refill her water bottle. She half expected Jim to scold her, take the bottle or the baby away, but he cheersed and said, gesturing over the rolled-out nylon, You ladies are welcome to share our tent. Plentya space in this baddie.

We don't want to impose, Calla said. You've already been so generous.

Jim said, I dig it. You need your space.

She hadn't thought of that. At home she had plenty of space, more solitude than even she needed, seemed like she could never escape it. But the crowded lot, the nearness of bodies, she'd need to zip herself away from it, for the nights at least, if she was going to survive the weekend.

Where was Audrey? Drifted off somewhere, probably taking bong hits with the neighbors and flashing that sideways smile of hers, leaving Calla, as always, with the logistics. She unrolled the mildewed canvas tent, unknotted the rope, staked the metal. Maneuvering with the baby— zonked out now, her face planted into curled fists—proved tough. By the time Calla finished, her beer had gone warm, Audrey still hadn't returned, and Reina squinted up at her from the grass where she sat fiddling with plastic baggies.

You've got the touch, she said. She almost never sleeps when I sling her.

Calla envied the slouch of her shoulders, her uninhibited movements, then thought how Reina must feel, unburdened for a little while. I can feel her heart beat, Calla said.

Reina tossed Calla a sticky looking, cookie-like lump wrapped in wax paper. She's got a strong one. That's what the midwife said.

What's this? Calla asked.

Ganga gooball, Reina said. My secret recipe. They're dreamy.

The lump tasted smoky, and sharp like old chocolate, gelatinous and mossy. Calla chewed and chewed, tried to swallow, chewed some more. And there was Audrey, her eyes all slyness. She plopped down beside Calla, accepting half of the gooball. She gulped it and wrinkled her nose. But Reina wasn't paying attention.

Let's explore, Calla said.

With the baby?

I don't want to disturb her, Calla said.

Let's not traipse around this place with you playing Mama Bear.

Parked a few sites off was an old school bus painted electric blue, three people in lawn chairs on the roof. Past it, in what Calla assumed was the direction of the stage, loomed an old air-traffic tower.

We should get a lay of the land, Calla said. I need to fill my water bottle.

I have water, Audrey said, shaking a sandwich bag filled with what looked like dusty bark. And mushrooms.

Calla said, I can go alone.

You know our rule.

Why do I need a buddy, but you don't?

I was just two tents over. Trip with me?

We eat them? Calla asked. The gooball filled her, spread warmth like sunning on a stone by the river. She closed her eyes and pictured the river tumbling past, dipping her toes in. Did the baby know how to swim? She'd have to ask Reina.

The guy said to mix it with something—peanut butter, or hummus.

We don't have either of those things. Calla leaned back on her elbows, letting the baby rest on her belly rather than pull against her shoulders.

We've got peanut butter, Reina said.

Audrey flung her arms wide. We're a match made in heaven. Let's make a sandwich.

Reina dug out the peanut butter, spread it with a plastic fork over slices of white bread. What's ours is yours.

Same, Audrey said. She sprinkled the mushrooms over each slice. Is this enough?

Looks it, Reina said. She folded the slices and handed one to Calla.

The pungent dryness repulsed her, and she could barely swallow, the whole mess like dirt-paste. Audrey's and Reina's lips puckered, too.

I hope this is worth it, Audrey said, grabbing Calla's beer and swigging the last sip.

Trust that it will be, Reina said. She gestured toward the baby. You okay with sleeping beauty for a while?

Calla nodded. Through their thin T-shirts, the baby's heart drummed steadily on.

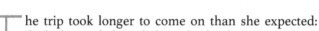

The trip took longer to come on than she expected: dusk descended, and then the landscape snapped, like a blind rolling up. Calla reached for the tube of grass and tents, anxious to tug it back—but no, that was Audrey's arm and Audrey's voice: *Calla, it's okay, I'm not going anywhere, you're hurting me* and then Calla was inside the tube, fire gleaming at the far end. She blinked into the tunnel. Blinking over and over till the dark tube wavered along the edges. Red. Pulsing. Thumpthumpthump. Slow whooshing rush. Blood red. A chamber. Sliding through, fire close at hand, thousands and thousands of heartbeats pounding into the night around her, echoing to the stars, which blinked in rhythm, skidding through the sky, and one falling, falling, so fast, right toward her, crashing into her chest at lightspeed. A whisper of new language, susurrations fluttering her chest like wings, like starlight, like so many heartbeats, like chaos being born.

Awash in a sea of drums, Calla drifted. She held Audrey's hand like it was an anchor, and Audrey said, Next stop: cosmic truth.

Too soon for a destination. Did she say that out loud?

Pass off that baby, Audrey said. We should sleep.

Calla looked around the fire. No Reina. Jim whirled like a dervish beyond the circle of light; he had been for hours. I like her, Calla said.

Audrey tried to loosen the sling.

Don't wake her, Calla said, clumsy in her attempt to

scoot away.

Audrey said, She's not yours.

Who said she was? Calla thought, looking again for Reina. Nowhere. The new beat inside her chest pounded. Audrey didn't seem to notice. She can sleep with us, Calla said. It'll be easier.

Audrey cast a glance at Jim, and back to Calla. I'd argue, but I'm too wiped.

Not that Jim stopped whirling, not when Calla stood near him, nor when she said, I've got the baby.

alla struggled through layers of sleep, like clawing her way through wet earth, her shirt heavy against her chest and stomach, toward the noise like a puppy whining to be let out.

The baby.

She jolted awake, untangling the sling to find the baby's face and thrashing fists, creased red flowers of fury. Fingers and arms weak, head bleary, Calla freed the baby. Her diaper was soaked, poop smeared down her bare legs, Calla's T-shirt, too.

Audrey, Calla said. Wake up.

Audrey mumbled, turned over, and buried her head in her sleeping bag.

Calla dug her foot into Audrey's leg, said, Help.

Audrey sat up and blinked bloodshot eyes at Calla. What is wrong with you?

Calla held out the wriggling baby. Not me.

Ah, shit. Audrey rubbed her face.

Literal shit. I need a fresh diaper.

And? Audrey flopped back into her sleeping bag.

You have to help.

Why?

Because I need you. And this was your idea.

What was?

Babysitting.

Audrey kicked off her sleeping bag. She glared at Calla and the baby, said, Nice set of lungs.

Diaper, Calla said. She could only hold the baby out like

this for so long; the screaming might shatter a window. If there were any windows nearby. Calla grabbed her poncho and went outside. The rain had come and gone and left a damp chill. She spread the poncho on the grass, set down the baby, fumbled with the stays. Fucking cloth, she thought, and cursed again when she got a look at the mess inside.

Audrey emerged, hoodie on, said, Dear God, it looks like that gooball. She let herself into Reina's and Jim's tent, emerged two minutes later with a patchwork bag and a white cloth. Is this it?

Looks like it, Calla said, taking the cloth. Hand me the wipes. A nasty rash spread along the baby's butt and thigh, but once cleaned, she relaxed, whining and sucking on her fingers, keeping her eyes on Calla with a look of wonder or suspicion or maybe mirth at how long everything was taking.

In Calla's hands, the white cloth felt thin, insubstantial. She couldn't see how or where it might tie. She should have paid more attention.

Maybe you need this, Audrey said, holding out a green diaper-shaped thing with Velcro tabs. Sure enough, inside was a pocket.

Calla folded and slid the cloth in, fastened the diaper. She's hungry, Calla said, scooping up the baby and patting her. And she needs fresh clothes.

Audrey rummaged around in the bag. There's some formula.

Just wake Reina up.

She isn't here.

What do you mean? Calla said.

Tent's empty is what I mean. Audrey started reading the formula instructions. We're going to need water.

Calla knocked the formula canister from Audrey's hand. The tent's empty? Where's Jim?

Audrey glanced at the surrounding tents. Nobody stirred. Then she picked up the formula, got a bottle and water, started mixing. I don't know, she said. We'll feed her, then we'll find them.

What happened last night?

You got weird, as usual.

Not me, Calla said. But the falling stars—

There were no stars, Audrey said. It rained. She handed Calla the bottle, and Calla wiggled the baby into the crook of her arm; the baby clamped on the nipple, her hands flexing and unflexing.

Let's call her Esther. She seems like an Esther, doesn't she? Calla said.

Audrey laughed. Sure she does. We find her on the fairground like some crazy doll—just like the song.

Esther's not the doll, Calla said.

Don't be so literal, Audrey said. Let's get her dressed and ready for—whoa. Audrey pulled a gallon-sized Ziploc of weed from the diaper bag.

Why am I not surprised that's in there? Calla looked down at Esther's serene face sucking at the bottle, her warm weight softening into Calla's arms. All trust and left to the mercy of strangers. Wasn't she too young for this? Calla stared into the sea of tents, wishing she had an answer. She said, Esther's a good name. It suits her.

Whatever you say. Audrey tossed Calla a onesie with umbrellas on it. This'll keep her covered, for now.

Calla'd never seen so many people. Stepping onto the vendor strip, she paused, wrapped her arms around Esther, said to Audrey, I'm not so sure about this.

Audrey loosened an arm, took Calla's hand. The baby seemed unbothered by the crowd. She craned her neck to see behind her, waved her arms, and squealed. Shirtless men grilled cheese sandwiches from the backs of station wagons; women with dreadlocks and armpit hair hawked hemp jewelry, calling, *Handmade, good juju.* A blond guy juggled oranges and apples; a couple clattered by on stilts. A herd of naked people rolled through, chattering. Easy in their skins. Calla prickled with heat and fatigue.

Audrey weaved them through crowds, struck up conversations with vendors, bought cheese sandwiches and blueberry muffins, questioned those who loomed out of the masses to admire the baby. Calla raked the crowds for Reina and Jim. But everyone looked the same: grubby, peaceful faces, patchwork and tie-dye, the whole mass a blobby amoeba stinking of old laundry. There was no shade anywhere. A guy walked by toting a kid on his back—the kid wore a sunhat and long-sleeves. Prepared. Unlike Esther, her ears and cheeks already flushed pink.

They walked and walked. Audrey said, There has to be some sort of lost and found on the lot. They can make an announcement.

Esther nuzzled at Calla's boob, and finding only cotton, took up whining. On what, an intercom? *Paging Jim and Reina. Please claim your baby.* Doubtful.

Do you have a better idea?

Calla shifted Esther and wiped the sweat off her stomach. Let's head back.

To the tent?

She's hungry, Calla said.

Audrey crossed her arms. Why didn't you bring the diaper bag?

Why didn't you?

Because I failed the egg assignment for us, remember?

Calla'd forgotten about the egg assignment, Audrey leaving their egg in the car one sunny May afternoon, hard-boiling it. Calla's first F, and in health class, of all things. She'd done extra credit to save her grade. She plucked at the sling strap and said, You haven't carried her at all. She's heavy.

Do I have to?

C'mon, Calla said. Help me out. We're supposed to be in this together.

We're supposed to be high as kites and dancing.

You're the one who said we'd take care of her.

You're the one who named her.

What does that have to do with anything?

You've been holding her since we got here.

Well, no one else is. Nausea welled in Calla; she wished she hadn't eaten the sandwich or the muffin. I didn't think they'd ditch her on us.

But you gave them the perfect opportunity.

Somehow this is my fault?

Who goes to a Phish show and ends up with a fucking baby? This is like an afterschool special or something.

I want to go home, Calla said.

Too bad, Audrey said.

God, you're a bitch, Calla said.

Audrey's eyes widened.

Calla glared.

Esther screamed, puncturing the space between them.

I knew this would happen, Audrey said.

Knew what would happen?

That you'd get all weird.

Then why did you spend three weeks convincing me to come?

You're my only friend brave enough to say yes, Audrey said, and her face softened. Let me carry her; we'll go back to the tent, feed her, and then go to the stage.

Calla tried to imagine the show—all these bumbling, zoned-out people carefree around her—keeping her elbows out, keeping Esther safe. We can't bring her to the show.

Audrey sighed. You're being ridiculous.

I'm being smart, Calla said. Something inside her flared. We should have been at the tent this whole time.

And miss out?

The only thing we're missing is this baby's parents. Please come back with me.

Nah, you're on your own, Audrey said.

How, Calla thought, is that any different than normal? She said, What about your buddy system?

Audrey pointed her chin toward the baby. You've got your buddy.

Fine, Calla said.

Fine, Audrey said. She crossed her arms and didn't budge when Calla walked away.

⁂

At the electric-blue school bus, Calla swung left and hurried through the tents to their spot.

She thought for a moment she had the wrong school bus. Until it registered: Jim's and Reina's tent was gone.

Calla stared at the matted-down grass. Turned in a circle. There was her tent. There was last night's firepit. The crumpled beer cans. The dingy camp chairs. Her legs trembled. Esther wailed as Calla sprinted toward the parking lot. Where was the Buick? Where? She remembered the hot-pink Vanagon they'd parked near—was it this row? No, here, the Vanagon with its plastic cluster of daisies stuck where the antenna should be. A few feet more. But the spot where the Buick should be parked gaped like a tooth that'd been punched out.

She dropped to her knees and placed her palms flat on the ground, gasping. This couldn't be happening. Esther smacked Calla's chest, frantic and angry. Calla struggled with the sling, got Esther loose. The baby howled, snot-smeared and confused and probably starving. Calla's heart hammered. What the hell, she thought, am I going to do?

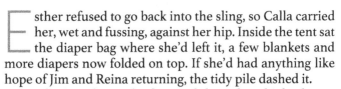

Esther refused to go back into the sling, so Calla carried her, wet and fussing, against her hip. Inside the tent sat the diaper bag where she'd left it, a few blankets and more diapers now folded on top. If she'd had anything like hope of Jim and Reina returning, the tidy pile dashed it.

Esther's rash raged a fiery red down her thighs, hot to the touch, and no diaper cream to be found. Calla fed her two bottles, tapped out a couple wet burps, watched Esther's drooping eyelids surrender to a nap. She'd have to wait for Audrey. The first set probably hadn't even begun yet. It could be hours.

She brought the diaper bag outside and spread its contents on the grass: Orajel, Polaroids of newborn Esther, handknit pink booties, organic nipple balm, the gallon Ziploc of weed, more diapers, formula, a battered copy of *The Velveteen Rabbit* with Reina's name scrawled on the first page in purple crayon. Nothing to go on—no phone numbers, no addresses, no hint of last names. She remembered Reina saying the baby'd been born on the dairy farm where Jim and she worked, up north, that the midwife had not reported the birth, so Esther could live entirely off the grid. Almost like she didn't exist.

Calla wondered if that made it easier to leave her behind.

She opened the Ziploc, the skunky waft like a slap. How

careless she'd been, foolish, to trust these people. The buds clung damp and gritty to her fingertips. She could sell it, use the money to get home with Esther. Home, she thought. Her grandmother's soft chin and teary eyes, and the thin set line of her mouth that didn't match the rest of her. She could roll herself a joint, escape her worry for a while; maybe she could nap beside Esther. She thought of Esther's eyes, how bright they were today on the lot, pupils no longer saucer-sized.

But yesterday Esther had a mother. The kind of mother who couldn't name her own baby. Still, wasn't that better than nothing?

Calla dropped the Ziploc into her lap. She didn't need the weed. If anything, she needed to get away from it. She had $100 in her pack, and so did Audrey, and together they could get Esther home. Surely someone would take pity on them, hitching with a baby, and offer a ride. Maybe all the way home. Or they could take the bus. If everything else failed.

A shirtless guy in baggy corduroys broke into Calla's thoughts, said, All alone? Come play. He brandished a Frisbee.

I can't, she said. I've got a baby.

Bring the baby, he said. We need a referee.

Calla said, She's sleeping. But hey, it's your lucky day. She tossed him the weed.

The guy assessed the bag, squinted at Calla. You're not a narc?

Consider it a payment on my karmic debt, she said.

Must've been quite an epiphany, he said, giving her a salute.

A little later, Esther burbled, and Calla found her waving her hands in the air, grinning. Calla knotted back her hair and scooped Esther up. All right, little girl, Calla said. You ready for your next big adventure? Esther bobbed her head, and Calla took it for a nod.

Calla'd packed everything by the time Audrey stumbled back covered in mud, a fog of booze and sweat rolling off her. Still with the baby, Audrey mumbled, not noticing the lack of tents.

We gotta go, Calla said. For hours she'd watched the star-spackled sky, listened to Esther breathe, counted heartbeats.

What are you talking about? Audrey said. It's the middle of the night.

They took off, Calla said. Jim and Reina. Their tent, their car. They're gone.

Audrey swayed and brought her hand to her mouth and chewed the skin of her thumb.

I have a plan, Calla continued, taking advantage of Audrey's speechlessness. If we leave now, I bet we can catch a ride with some non-campers.

Wait, you're not making any sense. What about the baby?

We're taking her home.

Home? Like to that dairy farm?

Home to Wardsboro.

Calla, she's not a puppy.

I know that, Calla said. I've thought it all out. She must have been left with us for a reason.

No, Audrey said. She crouched and unzipped her backpack.

I'll go without you, then.

Stop being crazy. Tomorrow we take her to the med station. They'll call the police, and they'll figure shit out. Now help me put the tent back up.

It's my tent. I'm taking it with me. Calla stood, hoisted her pack, the diaper bag.

Audrey groaned. This can't be happening.

It's happening, Calla thought.

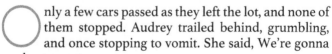

Only a few cars passed as they left the lot, and none of them stopped. Audrey trailed behind, grumbling, and once stopping to vomit. She said, We're gonna need more water soon.

Calla's shoulders and back ached, but they stopped to rest too often for her taste. The road stretched, unchanging, as dawn lit up the tree line.

Audrey said, Calla, I have to sleep. I'm gonna die.

Don't be melodramatic, Calla said, but she veered off the shoulder, and down a little incline into some woods. The leafy cover was like stepping into a church. Calla pushed back branches, forged ahead till she found a clearing. She handed off Esther, awake now, hungry again, to Audrey and erected the tent.

Not much formula left, Audrey said. We really need to hit a supermarket.

We'll feel better after we rest, Calla said.

They crawled into the tent and crashed into sleep.

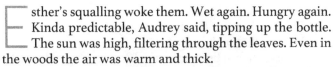

Esther's squalling woke them. Wet again. Hungry again. Kinda predictable, Audrey said, tipping up the bottle. The sun was high, filtering through the leaves. Even in the woods the air was warm and thick.

Calla pulled the directions from her pocket. In Caribou, we look for 1 South. After that, it'll be easy.

Is there a grocery store in Caribou? Audrey asked.

How should I know?

Audrey raised both eyebrows at Calla. You don't have to—

What? Know everything?

Be a jerk, Audrey said slowly.

Why am I always the responsible one?

You're the one who wants to keep the baby.

That's not what I mean, Calla said, her throat tight.

What, then?

For once, Calla thought, can't someone else know what to do? I need your help, Calla said.

I'm helping, Audrey said, standing, getting Esther into the sling. As best as I know how.

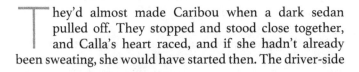

They'd almost made Caribou when a dark sedan pulled off. They stopped and stood close together, and Calla's heart raced, and if she hadn't already been sweating, she would have started then. The driver-side door opened, and a police officer climbed out.

Good evening, ladies, the officer said, striding toward them. In need of a ride?

Audrey looked at Calla, shook her head. We're walking.

Where to?

Home, Audrey said.

Were you up at the air-force base?

Calla rubbed Esther's back, prayed she wouldn't wake. She'd tied a bandana over her head to keep her from burning, and if she didn't fuss, maybe the officer would gloss over her, no questions asked.

Audrey said, We were there yesterday. But we left early. Too much.

I'd think it'd be tough, with a baby and all, the officer said.

Calla bit hard on the inside of her cheek.

Where's home? he asked.

Audrey tucked her hands into her pockets and looked at the pavement. Vermont.

The officer lifted his sunglasses, and leveled his steely eyes first on Audrey, then on Calla. Walking back to Vermont? How many miles you looking at?

Five hundred, Calla said. This much she knew; she tried to sound sure of herself, but her voice was hoarse, her throat dry.

The officer rubbed the bridge of his nose. You walk here?

We hitched, Calla said. She smelled the alcohol sweating out of Audrey.

With the baby? Without a car seat? The officer's eyes moved back and forth, waiting for their answer.

She's not ours, Audrey finally said.

The officer crossed his arms.

We hitched up here with this couple, and they asked us to babysit, Audrey said. Then they disappeared.

She's safe with us, Calla said. We're going to— but the way the officer rubbed his hand over his chin froze her.

How about I give you girls a ride to the station, and we get this sorted out?

Audrey pressed two fingers against Calla's thigh. Their all-clear.

Is that a yes? the officer asked. Or should I call backup?

That's a yes, Calla said.

⬤

Calla shivered on the metal chair, A/C cranked full blast and pouring from the vent overhead. Audrey sat stiff and uneasy, her eyes darting around the dull walls like she might find an exit and slip out unnoticed. Esther cried, her pink gums and pearl of a new tooth flashing, big tears rolling down her cheeks. Calla clutched her, rocked her, hummed a lullaby, trying to ignore the knot in her stomach.

They'd been searched. They'd been asked hundreds and hundreds of questions. They'd signed piles of paperwork. They'd made stilted phone calls home, Calla to her grandmother who sighed and asked, What on earth has gotten into you? Cold receiver against her mouth and ear, Calla said, I named her Esther. She could almost hear her grandmother clenching her jaw, thinking about what to say and coming out with, What do you need me to do? Calla wanted to cry, but she held back and said, Go down to the general store and sign some paperwork, then fax it back here. The dispatcher signaled for Calla to wrap things up, and she read out the return number. A foreign string of digits, bound to take her home. She tucked the slip of paper into her pocket.

The police let Calla keep Esther while they waited. In a district this large, it'd be a while before the social worker showed. Calla's spine pressed sharp and aching against the metal chair. Esther slept, and Audrey slept, but Calla could not. She stared at the concrete wall, trapped and helpless, everything out of her hands.

She fished *The Velveteen Rabbit* from the diaper bag and begged a pen from the dispatcher. Beneath Reina's name, she wrote: For Esther— Calla McDermott, 385 East Hill Rd, Wardsboro, VT 05355, 802-555-9806, and a small heart.

The clock hands ticked down the hours till the officer who'd picked them up returned to drive them to Presque Isle and put them on the bus. The morning dispatcher took Esther, told them not to worry—the social worker would be here soon, she'd be placed out, she'd be safe.

The officer stood outside his cruiser and waved to Calla and Audrey as they boarded, the only passengers this far north. It had been arranged that officers in Portland and Boston and Springfield would ensure their transfers, an officer from Wardsboro to meet them at the station in Brattleboro and escort them the final miles.

Calla dropped into a window seat and watched the low trees and yellow grasses roll away. How unknowable this place was, with a beauty she finally noticed: harsh and remote. She tried to imagine Esther growing up here, isolated, the questions she might ask, and no one to answer.

Audrey closed her eyes, said, You did good, Calla. Better than me, as usual.

It's not about that, she said.

Still.

Calla blurred her eyes over the landscape. Her arms and chest ached, offering no relief in their emptiness.

Frequency

The thing Sadie liked most about our house were the bats in the attic, and she wouldn't let me patch the hole they came and went by. After sunset, as an inky blue spread up the sky, out those creepsters came, wheeling around the backyard.

Temperatures spiked triple digits that summer, the hottest on record, but after darkness fell, the outside world became habitable. And Sadie, loosened by a few gins, seemed almost at ease those nights, curled in her Adirondack chair, sketching the bats as falling stars, as acrobats swinging from trapeze, as bombers on a suicide mission.

I watched her hand fly over the page from my chair, and I swirled my drink, said, Maybe it's time—

Sadie kept drawing but tilted her head toward me, a wave of hair hiding her face.

To start trying again. I sipped my drink. It's been a year.

Almost, she said.

You feel better, I said.

For the most part.

Have you changed your mind?

She stopped sketching and looked at me. A squirrel chattered. Strains of ballgame drifted from the neighbor's yard. Crickets sang. The bats whirred and clicked. One morning last summer, I'd found three of them hanging from the ceiling fan in my study. I wanted to trap them, but Sadie shushed me and shut the door and said, After dark. She disappeared into the other room and returned with her sketchpad. Still reeling from the second miscarriage, the shadows under her eyes looked like charcoal smudges.

They could have rabies, I said.

She said, Don't get bit.

That night, donning an old ski mask of mine to keep them out of her hair, she got all three outside in minutes.

Now, she flipped a page and said, I still want a family. Tipping the sketchbook so I could see, she drew two baby bats sleeping suspended from a skinny branch, wings wrapped tight like coffins.

A month passed without the heat abating, and everything I brought home from the farmers' market—kale, spinach, cucumbers and tomatoes, carrots, a bouquet of dahlias and daisies—looked wilted, listless, as Sadie unpacked the bags.

What are these for? she asked of the flowers.

They caught my eye.

She arranged them in a jar with her back to me. Barefoot, in her cut-offs and white tank top, bra-less—there was nothing unusual about this outfit, but her posture seemed different, her edges softened. Since the last miscarriage, if I even took her hand she pulled away. Never mind kissing the back of her neck, or stroking her thigh. I joined her at the counter.

Her hands still on the flower stems, she said, I'm about to ovulate. She turned to face me.

Does that mean—?

We should—before I lose my nerve, she said.

She loosened my tie. I ducked so she could pull it over my head. Halfway down my shirt buttons, she buried her face in my chest. I wrapped my arms around her, said, We don't have to, but she said, I want to. I tipped her chin upward. She smelled like her cedar soap and tasted like the little yellow tomatoes I'd just brought home. I slid my hands down her sides. Her hipbones had gone sharp, and it was almost a surprise, how easily she angled them toward me, winding her arms around my waist.

She said, In the bedroom, and I followed her up the stairs. She shed her clothes and perched on the edge of the bed, waiting for me to do the same, her eyes looking not at me, but out the window, the softening I'd sensed already slipping away. Still, she leaned back on her elbows and let me kiss down her stomach, over one thigh, before she squeezed my shoulder and motioned me up, to kiss her face. Her eyes were open, and we watched each other as she used her hand to guide me into her. She shifted her hips, whispered, *Derek*, like she used to, but when I pushed, her fingers gripped the sheet. I tried to get my hand beneath her lower back, to tilt her toward me, but she closed her eyes, said something I didn't catch, and rocked in a way I suddenly remembered—opening the door to that place we called our sun room.

For a moment we were drenched in the old bright warmth, and then the door swung shut.

I reached for her, but she was already pulling her shorts on. She swooped back, kissed me fast and light, left me thinking about her hair between my fingers and her legs wrapped around my waist. She hummed in the kitchen, opening the fridge, rustling bags. I heard her fill a pot with water, plink ice cubes into a glass.

Sadie said, after the second miscarriage, that she felt gutted. And I'd thought of an old house, stripped down to the studs, empty and waiting. The doctor told us she could find nothing physically wrong. To give it time. Miscarriages were more common than we realized.

After I showered, a gin and tonic waited for me on the kitchen counter, the news on the radio. Sadie diced radishes and cucumbers. I gentled the knife from her fingers and turned her around, asked, What can I do to help?

She pointed her chin toward the porch. The outside light needs to be replaced.

I was thinking more like—

Setting the table?

Sadie, I don't mean with dinner.

That screen on the porch still needs to be fixed. She returned to chopping.

I'll do the light.

On the ladder, I had a perfect vantage point of where the bats entered and exited the attic. Right above the nursery window. I hadn't been inside that room for months. Sadie kept the door closed.

When Sadie carried out the compost, I'd moved from the ladder onto the porch roof, assessing how I might patch the bats' hole, what materials I'd need. She squinted up at me, said: They call on multiple frequencies, you know. And they have these touch receptors on their wings to help them navigate air currents. She walked to the edge of the yard, emptied the bucket of scraps. On her way back in, she said, I wish you'd let them be, Derek. Dinner's ready.

Sadie lay on the bed when I got home the next afternoon, clad only in a pair of ruffled, blue satin underwear. Sunlight fell through the drawn blinds in long slashes.

You okay? I asked.

She said to the ceiling, My fertility window is still open.

When I didn't move, she sat up and unzipped my pants. The A/C was off, and I was sweating. I unbuttoned my shirt, and Sadie watched. Even though she was already naked, as I pulled my undershirt over my head, I grew nervous. I stood there, about to say, Are you certain? but she tugged my wrist, and we lay down facing each other, and my hand was on the curve of her waist, and Sadie was smiling—really smiling, the edges of her eyes crinkling—and I couldn't remember the last time I'd seen that. She threw her leg over my hip, she didn't need to guide me this time, there were no locks to fumble. Just that open space, the two of us inside it, and her hand on my back urging me deeper, until the rays of light filtering through the blind blurred, and we slipped apart, Sadie's breath moist against my shoulder.

She said, Will you get me some water?

I filled the glass, wondering how long it'd been since she'd said, Hold me or That was nice or I love you. What she would do if I said one of those things. If I should try.

Back in the bedroom, Sadie had her legs up the wall, a pillow beneath her hips, eyes closed, hair fanned out. She reached for the glass, set it on her stomach. I sat next to her, and she moved, just a little, away.

Did you have a good day? I asked.

Mm-hmm, she said. I sold one of the bat drawings.

I tried to picture Sadie's bats, framed, hanging in a stranger's house, and all that came to mind were those twin babies, the way she'd shaded the thin skin of their wings, the peaceful expression she'd given their faces. Which? I asked.

You know that barista at MetalMug—the one with the tattoos?

Sadie knew I knew her—it was hard to miss those catlike eyes and inked-up arms. For a while I'd noticed Sadie studying her in this too-curious way, and I'd asked about it, sort of a joke, but Sadie'd gone serious and said, Derek, please, but I didn't see her looking again after that. Whenever I went in alone, the woman offered only a blank stare.

She can afford art?

Will you let me finish? She's friends with the people at that skydiving place in Orange. They wanted the parachutists.

How—?

She saw me working on it one afternoon, Sadie said.

That's great, I said.

She made a low noise in her throat.

What?

Don't sound too excited, she said.

I mean it. I'm proud of you.

Her eyes blinked open, and she looked at me upside down. Proud?

Sadie shook me awake. There's a bat stuck on the porch, she said. I need your help.

I glanced at the clock. What are you doing up?

We have to get it out before it gets light.

I buried my face in the pillow. Call animal control.

She sighed. A few seconds later, I heard her rustling in the downstairs closet, a clatter of stuff falling. The porch door creaked open and shut. I was tired, tired of bats, inside and out. Grumbling, I went down to the kitchen.

Through the window, I watched Sadie—my bicycle helmet on her head, a broom in one hand, and a sheaf of newspaper in the other—crouch opposite the screen where the bat hung, her mouth moving. Talking to the thing. She'd torn the broken screen behind her halfway down. She tapped below the bat with the broom handle; the bat let go, flew in tight circles around the porch. Sadie stood, brought the newspaper up and whooshed the bat forward. It flapped past the window frame and into open air. Lucky creature.

Sadie removed the bicycle helmet, hugging her arms around her body. I opened the porch door, and the squeak broke Sadie's smile. She turned, startled.

I said, Home run.

She said, I'll fix the screen later.

sat in my office, unable to shake the image of that bat sailing into the dawn, Sadie's triumphant smile, how she hugged herself, how she dodged past me into the living room. Shaking her head when I said, Why don't you come back to bed?

I pulled up the plans for the new school building I needed to finish, but I couldn't concentrate. I clicked over to the Internet, Googled bats. Lots of stuff I already knew came up: potentially rabid, not bloodsuckers despite the vampire-myth, echolocation, mosquito eaters. I read several articles about the devastation of white-nose syndrome, entire hibernating colonies wiped out. An advertisement for bat houses ran up the side of one page, and after a few clicks, I arrived at a build-your-own bat house site. A decent compromise, I thought, studying the simple sketches. Our trees were tall enough. I had the tools. Something I could live with. I printed the plans.

I brought them home to show Sadie, preparing a spiel to win her over, the houses and relocation a project to work on together.

But she'd gone out. The note magneted to the fridge read: *home around 8. i'll get takeout. s.*

Which gave me three hours. More than enough time to bike to the lumberyard, pick up scraps, grab a bottle of wine, have it all laid out and ready by the time Sadie walked in.

On my ride back—wood, wine, and a book on bats tucked in my panniers—I saw Sadie's Volkswagen parked in a spot outside MetalMug. I slowed, wheeled my bike up to the rack, looking for Sadie through the plate-glass. There, toward the door, her back to me. She had on an old baseball T-shirt of mine, the screen-printed 13 cracked and peeling.

And sitting across from her was the barista, two nose piercings, cropped dark hair, osprey with spread wings tattooed across her chest.

I stopped.

They huddled toward each other. The barista wiped her cheeks. She reached across the table and rested her hand on Sadie's. Sadie brought the barista's hand to her mouth, pressing her lips to its palm. After a moment, the barista drew her hand away and stood, disappearing behind the employees-only door. Sadie dropped her head, hair falling like curtains.

I got on my bike and rode home.

***

Sadie returned an hour later and stood in the doorway of my study holding a bag of takeout. Did you go for a ride?

I did, I said. Where were you?

The library, she said. Reading about bats.

That's a coincidence, I said.

Her hand clenched the paper bag, and her eyes darted to the floor before meeting mine.

I was there, too—researching bat houses.

Why?

So they'll have a place to live, I said.

Don't be ridiculous. They have a place to live.

Not in the attic. It isn't safe, once we have the baby—

There's no baby.

I tapped my pencil on the plans I'd printed. We have to get some exclusion devices, make sure we evacuate them all.

There's nothing wrong with where they are.

I dropped the pencil and crossed my arms. We move them, or I call the exterminator.

Sadie straightened, her jaw tight. She said, I got you dumplings and pork fried rice.

I'm not very hungry, I said.

Fine, she said. I'll put it in the fridge.

S adie left the open box of tampons on the back of the toilet, so I didn't need to ask whether our attempts had been successful. At dinner, I said, We'll keep trying, and Sadie nodded, not looking at me.

The same thing happened the next month.

When we needed coffee, I went to a new café.

Sadie didn't leave the house much—she spent a ton of time drawing, headphones on. I built seven bat houses but left them stacked on my workbench in the basement. On Sadie's art table in the living room, her sketches piled up. After dinner, even as the nights turned crisp, she sat in the Adirondack and drew more bats.

I stopped joining her. I have work to do, I told her. A few times, I riffled through her stuff—but nothing seemed unusual, nothing looked like proof.

One morning Sadie climbed into bed, pulled me toward her. Don't tell me we have another bat, I said.

My basal temp's high, she said.

Are we—?

But she covered my mouth with hers, and she didn't seem to mind that I barely woke up.

That night she followed me to bed, undressing with me, the whole thing quick and quiet. The next morning, finding her still beside me, I nuzzled into her neck, but she tensed, said, Yesterday was enough.

And then one night, I startled awake, Sadie gone from bed. She wasn't on the porch or at her art table or outside. Climbing the stairs to get my phone—my stomach in knots —I noticed the nursery door ajar. Sadie sat in the middle of the room, legs folded lotus-style, and without opening her eyes she said, Please, so I pulled the door shut and spent the rest of the night staring at the ceiling, alone.

I called out of work in the morning. Sadie left for a meeting, and I went into the baby's room. The maple crib that'd been mine, the hummingbird mobile we'd bought, the white basket full of our battered copies of *Holly Hobbie's Nursery Rhymes* and *Make Way for Ducklings* and *Goodnight Moon*—everything exactly as I remembered.

But tacked to the wall above the light switch was an

unframed drawing I'd not seen before—a bat in a buggy, its wrinkled face peering over the edge at two figures in the distance. Intricate crosshatching and exquisite swirls done in black India ink. Unsigned, but definitely not Sadie's. Along the bottom edge ran an indentation from writing on the other side. I wiggled the tack from the wall and flipped the paper: *may all you wish for find you. with love.*

Above, the bats slept. I wondered what Sadie would do if she found the drawing gone. But I stuck it back in place, pushed the tack down, and shut the door.

In the basement, I piled the bat houses into some crates and carried them out to the yard. I got the ladder from the shed, but couldn't bring myself to climb up.

That night, I put on a sweatshirt and poured a drink and joined Sadie. She barely glanced at me, kept tapping her pencil against the paper propped on her lap: a stippling of marks like a cluster of dark stars.

She nodded toward the sky: Full moon.

How are you feeling?

The same, she said.

As the moon? I wanted to ask. I sipped my whiskey, said, Do you want a drink? but she shook her head. At the top of her sketchpad, she shaded a large circle and below it added a small house. Our house.

I brought up the bat houses, I said.

I saw them. You did a nice job.

Now's the time, before they hibernate.

I'm worried.

They'll be okay.

They fly by feel, she said. What if the houses don't feel right?

I thought they used echolocation.

That, too. She flipped the pages of her sketchbook, stopping on a page where she'd drawn two big bats sitting in lawn chairs, lowball glasses on the table between them. They're not bothering us, she said.

What about those in the study? The one on the porch?

Sadie made a noise, half laugh, half growl. They were here first.

This is our house, Sadie. I'd like it to be safe.

I didn't want this house, she said.

You never told me that.

Because I knew you wanted it.

It's a good house, I said. Perfect for us.

But you don't like the bats in the belfry, she said. She set down her pencil and watched the bats flit and dive.

I saw you, I said. At MetalMug.

Sadie took a deep breath.

How long? I said.

She shook her head.

A month? Two?

I ended it.

But her drawing is upstairs in our baby's room.

Sadie folded her hands over her heart.

Are you in love with her?

She understood things.

I tried to, I said. I wanted to.

I know, she said, but it felt like I didn't exist anymore. That I was uninhabitable space.

That's not true.

It's how I felt.

And now?

I'm here.

In the house you never wanted.

She tore a piece of paper from her book and offered it to me; in the shadowy dark, I made out a little bat, curled inside a larger bat's belly.

For the baby's room.

It's not finished, she said, taking the drawing back. She outlined another bat, folding its wing around the pregnant one. I have an ultrasound next week.

An ultrasound?

She nodded. It's still early. But I can feel how strong it is.

Flying by feel. How else.

Will you come with me—to the appointment?

If you want me there, I said.

She said, I do.

Beholden

met Tommy outside the all-night grocery. Three a.m., me standing with a six-pack in one hand, digging for matches with the other, cigarette unlit in my mouth. Kellie said, Tommy, this is Annabelle, and we shook, and he held my eyes longer than necessary and said, Ah, so you're Kellie's elusive roommate.

Smoke forgotten, fatigue forgotten, neighborhood forgotten—for a split second only this new person zoomed into focus: froggy smile, round wire-rimmed glasses, red hoodie.

Kellie said, Tommy, join us for a beer?

They were in History of Religion in America together, and Kellie had what she called an inconsequential crush on him. I knew he majored in Comparative Lit, that he came from Buffalo, that his mother painted landscapes. He lived on the sixth floor of our complex. His shopping bags bulged with frozen pizzas and cereal boxes.

He said, I'd love to.

Kellie pulled a lighter from her pocket and sparked it.

I didn't break Tommy's stare while I lit my cigarette. Then I looked away, down the three blocks to where the wreckage of the Towers still smoldered, and said, C'mon, let's go.

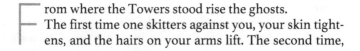

rom where the Towers stood rise the ghosts.
The first time one skitters against you, your skin tightens, and the hairs on your arms lift. The second time,

you return to your apartment and get under the blankets and think you are coming down with the flu. There is no such thing as ghosts, you whisper.

But the ghosts don't need your belief. In the deserted streets, they are learning to inhabit their new formlessness; they are soaking up the heat and the ash. They come especially at that hour when it is neither dark nor light, and they hover. You will want to draw back the heavy sky, to release them. But it would be no use.

They are beholden to this ground.

***

A t 7 a.m. Tommy winked and said, Goodnight ladies, and showed himself out.

Kellie said, He likes you, before shutting her bedroom door.

I perched alone on my loft bed, smoking through half a pack of Camel Reds. There were ashes in the air, ashes in my mattress, ashes in my shoes, in the pages of my books, in my hair. Every breath I took.

A few hours later there was a knock at the door, and Tommy stood, wearing the same outfit he'd had on before, and he said Hi, and I said Hi, and I let him in, and he said, I like your pants. He rested a hand on my hip, ran his thumb along the purple velvet.

I said, Do you want some coffee?

He said, I'd love some coffee.

Kellie slept on, through coffee, through a half-dozen badly scrambled eggs, through my hasty reading of "The Waste Land," through my rush to get ready for Modern American Poetry.

Tommy waited in the kitchen while I showered and dressed, and when I came out from behind the curtain that cordoned off my room from the living space, he said, Your hair looks different.

I said, It's clean now.

He said, It looks good. But I could tell he liked it better dirty.

Do you have class, too? I asked.

I have some stuff to do at the library, he said. When's

your class over?

Seven.

How about dinner?

That sounds nice, I said, shrugging on my peacoat. Do you need anything from your place?

No, I have everything.

You travel light, I said.

Unlike you, he said, lifting my messenger bag from the floor and handing it to me.

We walked down the eight flights of stairs into the lobby, where he opened the front door, waved me through.

You don't need to do that, I said.

I like to, he said.

We stepped out into the over-warm afternoon. The sky was a heavy, flat white, and the air stuck to our skin.

Y ou call your neighborhood The Inferno.

Which circle?

The first.

All night long dump trucks grumble through the narrow, cobbled streets, carting away warped steel, shattered glass, charred bits of filing cabinets. You have no idea what they do with the bones, the teeth, the wedding bands. You sit in your window, listening to the groan of cleanup, and you blow smoke rings into the darkness.

Under no circumstance will you speak the words Ground Zero.

T ommy stood waiting on the front steps of the University Center with a bouquet of maroon carnations when I got out of class. For you, he said, thrusting them into my hands.

I tucked the flowers under my arm, tapped out a cigarette. Before I could search for a lighter, Tommy had one flared and waiting. You want? I asked, holding out the pack.

I quit, he said. How about that diner on Eighth?

Sure, I said.

He ordered a burger.

I said, I'm a vegetarian.

He said, Of course you are.

I said, What's that supposed to mean?

He said, You're kind of an ascetic, aren't you?

I said, Not exactly.

Are you going to order something? The waiter stood at our table, pencil poised.

English muffin, I said. Dry. And a coffee, black.

See, Tommy grinned, pinning me with his eyes.

I didn't ask him to stop. His gaze tethered me, made me feel necessary.

Tell me something, he said.

I need tampons. But I'm broke.

I'll steal some for you.

My favorite chore is laundry, I said. I picked up a napkin and folded it into a crane.

You can do mine, he said. I flicked the napkin-crane at him, and he caught it, set it down by his wallet.

We sat at a table by the window, and beyond our reflections, people rushed past. I thought about how quickly the city had slid back to breakneck and careless. There were still candlelight vigils in Union Square and Missing posters papering the subway stations, tattering at the edges. But no more eye contact. No more fellowship. The waiter arrived with my coffee and a vanilla malted milkshake.

Tommy pushed the milkshake toward me, said, Let's share.

I said, I don't like milkshakes.

You're crazy. He spooned some into his mouth. He said, Do you think there's a God?

No, I said.

I figured, he said.

I raised my eyebrows and sipped my coffee. It was bitter, old.

He said, Last night when I saw you, I thought, Anyone who wears that much black couldn't possibly believe in God.

I n the beginning, God created the heaven and the earth. Nowhere in *Genesis* does it say God created ghosts. Yet, still they brush over your skin, riffle your hair. Still they settle into your bowls and spoons, drift past the light-bulb you read by.

They filter into your dreams invited or not, and so you fold back your duvet and plump your pillow in welcome.

T ommy wasn't a terribly good kisser, but he had strong hands. He seemed to operate by instinct only, and his body spoke the language of desire: force and craving. The morning after the diner, the morning after the night he first kissed me, I woke and found him gone. My thighs, my stomach, my throat, unfurled, my skin tender and sore. I bit my lip and buried my face in my pillow and thrilled a little.

Kellie snored, her bedroom door open, the steady noise filling the apartment. I'd heard her come in late, after Tommy curled around me, his face pressed against my hair. I'd kept my eyes closed, listening as Kellie rummaged in the fridge. I knew she was pinching pats of butter and letting them melt in her mouth. I knew she would shuffle over and push back the curtain and peek into my room.

Lips still tingling, I dragged myself out of bed, and snapped up the blind. On my desk, next to a stack of books, sat the largest box of tampons the drugstore sold and a fresh pack of smokes and a tiny cast-iron skillet holding down a note: *this isn't for your eggs. t.*

In the bathroom, bedsheet in a puddle at my feet, my body looked as if I'd encountered a wild, biting animal. I remembered the carnations, forgotten in the diner.

The radiators clacked and banged, and we kept all the windows in the apartment open—muggy air on both sides, not right for this time of year—but I wore a turtleneck anyway.

Kellie emerged from her room groggy and grumpy and poured a cup of coffee and sat at the card table we used in the kitchen, and with a sweep of her eyes, said, That didn't take long.

You wend your way to the makeshift memorial, carrying a clutch of crimson and yellow snapdragons. Already so many flowers are piled there, wrapped in cellophane, explosions of orange, pink, red. You get to your knees on the sidewalk on Broadway and press your forehead to the cement. Grit studs your skin. You do not pray. You do not whimper or sob. The ghosts are young, confused, and hungry, and they will not be pacified. You breathe deeply, gather the air into your lungs, hold it there.

Kellie called the pot dealer—that was her job. The way it worked was she dialed the number and asked for Aunt Linda. An hour or so later, the doorman buzzed us: John's here to see you.

My job was to go down and sign John in, the doorman looking the other way, out toward the sidewalk. Drizzle clouded the air, and John didn't wear a coat over his T-shirt. Around his neck was a tangle of gold chains, among them a medal of St. Sebastian.

I sniffled and pointed to the elevator, said, Eighth floor.

John said, Where you going?

I take the stairs, I said.

I'll take them, too, he said.

He wheezed as we climbed, though I was the one with the cold, a cough rattling my chest.

You sound bad, girl, he said.

I feel like shit, I said. But I'll live.

You gotta make yourself a hot toddy.

What's that?

You ain't never drank a hot toddy? Where you from?

Massachusetts, I said.

John harrumphed. You brew up some ginger tea, squeeze in a lemon, spike it with brandy. Cures what ails. A coughing fit overtook me, and John paused, leaning against the concrete wall. You claustrophobic? he asked.

We're almost there, I said. One more flight.

Once inside the apartment, he said, Nice place you got

here. He glanced toward the window. Considering.

Kellie flirted and haggled with him over the price of the buds while I did yesterday's dishes.

Before he left, John called over, Don't forget, girl. Hot toddy. You'll be good as new. He smiled, revealing a gold eyetooth.

I raised my hand in a wave.

Kellie said, That's classic. But she left to buy brandy and lemon, then boiled the water and brewed the tea. She made one for both of us, half brandy at least, though she wasn't sick.

When I told Tommy about John and the hot toddy, he grabbed me by the wrists, his hands completely enclosing them, and said, When's the last time you ate a proper meal?

I had soup earlier, I said.

From a can?

From the deli.

Hot toddy, he said, shaking his head. You're so damn innocent. What happened to your eyebrows?

I burned them lighting a cigarette off the stove.

He winced, pulled me closer, placed his lips on the singed hair. He said, Try not smoking for a day or two. Give your lungs a chance to actually breathe.

I thought, Who's the innocent one here?

On your birthday, you walk at midnight to the barrier blockading the site. A young woman in a camel-hair coat joins you, her hands laced through the chain-link. Despite the late hour, her mouth glistens with red lipstick. She turns, asks, Why? Before you can answer, before you can skitter away, she embraces you: five minutes, ten, until eternity seems too long, and then she is gone.

It was Tommy who bought the ecstasy. Who broke the tab in half and placed it on my tongue. Who said, I can't explain it, but you'll know when you start rolling.

It took longer than I expected. We left his place for mine.

Kellie came out of the bathroom, hair done, face made-up. She was going to dinner with her aunt; there was a cab waiting downstairs. She said, I'll be drinking expensive champagne, which should alleviate some of the boredom.

She hugged me goodbye, which I didn't expect. That's when it hit.

She said, I'll see you two tomorrow.

I closed my eyes. What is that? I said.

It's your clothes against your skin, Tommy said. He tied back the curtain-door, switched off the overhead light, leaving just the glow of twinkle lights Kellie and I had strung all around my room, the kitchen, the hallway.

Seems so much bigger in here, I said. I trailed my fingers along my dresser, the wood grain, the cold metal pull. From one of my drawers, I unearthed a blanket, and spread it on the floor. Come here, I said. Beneath my palms the fleece radiated electric softness.

We lay on our backs, our bodies magnetized shoulder to foot, staring at the ceiling as if stars might appear and pull us up and pierce us to the tapestry of sky.

Being in your apartment is like being inside a Christmas tree, Tommy said.

And this blanket is our nest, I said.

He intertwined his fingers with mine, tugging so I faced him. When we kissed, he took my bottom lip between his teeth and bit.

I said, Let's never leave.

He said, You'd tire of that fast.

＊

At a house party in Brooklyn, a friend brings you into his room, closes the door to the music and chatter. From behind a pile of books, he retrieves a glass jar. Inside is a pair of eyeglasses, one lens gone, one lens cracked, coated in grime. He turns the jar so the dust upheaves and swirls, like a snow globe. He hands it to you, and when you cradle it in your palm, light pulses through the lens and you gasp. He says, Don't tell.

＊

After the holidays, a cold snap turned the sky to flint. Kellie'd gone home for break, and I paced the apartment, my window open a crack to blow smoke out of. After a few days of waiting, I went downstairs and knocked on Tommy's door.

He answered, said, Oh, you're here, I didn't realize. Though he knew I'd only be out of town for a week, same as him.

Can I come in?

He hesitated. I'm about to get lunch. He backed into the apartment, and I followed him, the door banging shut. I'm going to Burger King, he said. Then I have stuff to do.

I said, I'll go with you. I could use the air.

Fine, he said. Where's your coat?

Upstairs.

I'll meet you in the lobby, he said.

We walked, he a little faster than I, toward Broadway.

It'll snow soon, I said.

You think, he said.

I listened to the weather, I said.

I got a table while Tommy ordered. He sat and unwrapped his food, and I studied the people around us—a girl younger than me bottle-feeding a baby; an old man in a newsie cap; two cleanup workers huddling over their trays, the fluorescent lights magnifying the shadows beneath their eyes, the corners of their mouths pinched down. I wanted to be anywhere but here.

Tommy ate his Whopper, watching the wall of televisions behind me, before he said, How long have we been seeing each other?

I counted back, said, Two months next week. Why?

Because I don't want to anymore, he said. He shoved the last bite into his mouth, finally focusing on me as he chewed.

There's no arguing with that, is there, I said. I grabbed a napkin and folded it into a loose cherry blossom.

He plucked it from my hands, examined it, let it flutter down onto his tray. You're an unusual girl, he said.

Did I do something wrong?

He removed his glasses and wiped them and put them back on. I'm just—not feeling this anymore.

You don't get points for honesty, I said and crossed my

arms over my chest.

He said, Are you ready to go?

I said, I'll stay here.

He stood and walked out.

I moved to where Tommy had been sitting. The TVs were all tuned to the same channel. On the screens a blond woman with upswept hair stood beside images of the Towers belching smoke, her hands and mouth moving without sound. Then images of Afghani men with kufi on their heads crouching on desolate earth. A ticking scroll of names and numbers beneath.

For a long time, I watched the frames flicker and repeat. The thing that transfixed me was the smoke, how it billowed, blackening the air. How the people stepping out of it covered in ash appeared so unsolid that an exhale might blow them away. How that dust still hung suspended in the air, how it slipped into the slimmest of spaces. How it clung to each of us.

Back outside, enormous snowflakes blew down like scraps of paper. I stood and let them pelt my cheeks. Then I lit a cigarette and, bowing my head, made for home.

L ast suitcase packed, set by the door, you drift through the empty apartment, one final sweep. Running your fingertips along the windowsill, you think you will not miss this place. You will not miss this dust.

But the ghosts have become hitchhikers. You will discover them unpacking in another borough, another city, another state. They prefer the folds of hoodies, the grooves of shoe soles, the corkscrew and bottle opener. They travel light, with no particular destination.

Ghosts are like seeds that way, and they've sewn themselves into you.

Your body a field ripe for planting.

You wait, biding your time, until you burst into bloom.

Sara Rauch's fiction and essays have appeared in *Paper Darts*, *Hobart*, *Split Lip*, *So to Speak*, *Qu*, *Lunch Ticket*, and other literary magazines, as well as in the anthologies *Dear John, I Love Jane; Best Lesbian Romance 2014;* and *She's Lost Control*. She has covered books for *Bustle*, *BitchMedia*, *Curve Magazine*, Lambda Literary, *The Rumpus*, and more. In 2012, she founded the literary magazine *Cactus Heart*, which ran through 2016. She holds an MFA from Pacific University. Sara teaches writing at Pioneer Valley Writers' Workshop and Grub Street and also works as an independent editor and manuscript consultant. *What Shines from It*, which won the Electric Book Award, is Sara's first book. She lives with her family in Holyoke, Massachusetts. Find her online at sararauch.com, on Twitter at @sararauch, and on Instagram at @sara__rauch.

Author Thanks

Thank you to the team at Alternating Current Press—particularly Leah Angstman, Eric Shonkwiler, Paige Ferro—for all their hard work in giving this collection a home in the world.

To my Pacific University friends: Emilie Rohrbach, Jen Murvin, Tas Condie, Hillary Mohaupt, Hilary Bilinski, and Killian Czuba; and to my Pacific advisors: Christine Sneed, the late Katherine Dunn, and Pete Fromm; and to all the other writers I've worked with over the course of my education—thanks for believing in me and for helping me hone my words into something I'm proud of.

A million thank yous to Kate Sheeran Swed for reading these stories over and over, and for cheering me on every time I need it. If I've ever known a generous, kind, bighearted reader, it is she.

Thank you to my mom and dad, Doreen and Chris, for a lifetime of support, and to my brother, Matthew, for moving my rather large library at least 15 times, and to my "sister-in-law," Christine Przewoznik, for her boundless enthusiasm. Thank you to Lee Marino Biase for 30+ years of friendship, laughs, advice, and killer headshots. Thank you to Sarah Johnson Court for all the epic drives and musical adventures, including the one that inspired "Free." Thank you to Meegan Schreiber for coffee dates and long walks. Thank you to Moira Megargee for all the book talk. Thank you to Sasha Starr, who held space for me while I dreamed many of these stories into existence. Thank you to my Pinch crew—Leah Hughes, Joyce Rosenfeld, Amy Breiteneicher, Marcia Gordenstein, and Jena Sujat—for embracing my crazy schedule so that my writing could take first priority. And no list of thanks would be complete without my cats—Greta, Oskar, and Michou—who keep me grounded, accountable, and strangely inspired.

And last but not least, though they came onto the scene after these stories were written, I am ever grateful to my sons, Theodore and Christopher; my stepson, Oliver; and my husband, Steve, for being the best family on earth: you've made my wildest dreams come true.

Acknowledgments

The author wishes to thank the following publications where previous versions of these stories were first published:

"Secondhand" first appeared in *So to Speak*.

"Answer" first appeared as "Aleta Alehouse" in *FictionFix*.

"Addition" first appeared in *Sinister Wisdom*.

"Abandon" first appeared as "A State of Abandon" in *Wilde Magazine*.

"Kitten" first appeared in *Rock & Sling*.

"Kintsukuroi" first appeared as "What Shines from It" in *Qu*.

"Free" first appeared as "Esther" in *Eleven Eleven*.

"Frequency" first appeared in *WomenArts Quarterly*.

Colophon

The edition you are holding is the First Edition of this publication.

The cursive font used throughout the book is Rosabelia Script, created by SolidType. The bold letters of the cover title are DIN, created by Albert-Jan Pool. The sans-serif font on the back cover and front cover quotation is Avenir, created by Adrian Frutiger. All other sans-serif typeface throughout the book is Alcubierre, created by Matt Ellis. All standard interior text is Athelas, created by José Scaglione and Veronika Burian. The Alternating Current Press logo is Portmanteau, created by JLH Fonts. All fonts are used with permission; all rights reserved.

Front cover artwork: "Never Before." Back cover artwork: "Life Poem." Artwork by Loui Jover, ©2020. Find him on Instagram at @louijover, at saatchiart.com/louijover, and on Facebook at facebook.com/lojoverart. Artwork is used with permission; all rights reserved. Cover design by Leah Angstman.

The coffee cup, flask, and wine glass were created by Any Li. The burrito and chips were created by Everysunsun. The half-sun divider graphic was created by Leah Angstman. The owl was modified by Enliven Designs. The mouse was created by Bonitas Art, and the teacups were created by Love Watercolor, both modified by Leah Angstman. The eggplants and the hot toddy were created by Andry and Vadim at MyStocks. The lilacs were created by Natalia Piacheva, and the Mason jar was created by Lary at Art Insider, both modified by Leah Angstman. The black kitten was created by Cheng at Cornercroft. The vases were created by Kaleriiat. The teddy bear was created by Aneta at Old Continent Design. The bat was created by Watercolor Fantasies. The wedding rings were created by Rich Stoker, and the ashes were created by Leah Angstman.

The Alternating Current lightbulb logo was created by Leah Angstman, ©2013, 2020 Alternating Current. Sara Rauch's photo was taken by Lee Biase, ©2020. All material is used with permission; all rights reserved.

All of these books (and more) are available at
Alternating Current's website: press.alternatingcurrentarts.com.

ALTERNATINGCURRENTARTS.COM

CPSIA information can be obtained
at www.ICGtesting.com
Printed in the USA
BVHW031733030221
599297BV00003B/55